HIDDEN DANGER

Book Five of The Hidden Saga

Amy Patrick

Oxford South Press/ May 2016
Cover design by Cover Your Dreams
Formatting by Polgarus Studio

For my Hidden Honeys—the incredible readers who love my books and give me so much encouragement every day! You mean the world to me.

CONTENTS

CHAPTER ONE
NOT FOR US

The blood rushed to my head, making it hard to think.

All I knew was one minute I was sitting at one of the three stoplights in this dinky little town, and the next my car was being blown across the intersection as if it was a cardboard paper towel tube rolling in a windstorm.

I wasn't hurt—at least I didn't think I was. I was still strapped into my seatbelt. In fact, it constricted my chest and ribs uncomfortably as I hung suspended from it, my hair in my eyes, my trembling hands still clenching the steering wheel.

Trying to get my bearings and figure out what was going on, I glanced to the right—*oh God*. The passenger side was crushed. That's why the car was tilted to one side. I seemed to be in the one pocket of the front seat that remained intact.

Chunks of glass protruded from the frame of the windshield like the few remaining teeth in a bare-knuckle fighter's mouth. Through the opening, the upside-down view of the street portrayed a chaotic scene. Debris was strewn across the road—things that did not look like car parts. And people running. Everything looked orange. Maybe I had a head injury after all. No—the orange glow was fire. I could smell it.

Something—a building, or maybe a huge truck—was engulfed in flames. I could feel the heat of it, though I didn't have a clear view of exactly what had exploded. Yes—an explosion. That was what it was. Had to be. I remembered something slamming the car, rocking it up onto two wheels. And then, just as the car righted itself again, another blast hit and sent me rolling side-over-side.

Maybe one of those big fuel trucks had crashed into a power pole and blown up. I strained to see more but in my restricted, and increasingly uncomfortable, position, I couldn't spot what was burning. What if it *was* a fuel truck and it was right next to me? My car could catch on fire, too. That thought brought me out of my dazed state and spurred my heart rate into an agitated clip.

I need to get out of here.

Pressing one hand against the ceiling for support, I fumbled for my seatbelt clasp, pressed the button. Nothing. Ugh. It was stuck or something.

There was a metallic screech as someone wrenched open my car's door, which now that I was looking at it was oddly bent.

"Ava? Ava!" Asher's face peered through the opening, shockingly pale and creased with concern. His sea-blue eyes were huge and wild. Then his expression relaxed. "Oh thank God you're alive. When I saw your convertible on its top…"

Elation and relief rushed through me in a cool stream. "Hi," I said. "Can you get me out? My head feels like a water balloon that's about to burst." My voice was shaky. Before I'd seen his face, there had been no tears threatening, but now it was all I could do not to lose it.

"You bet. Just hold on a minute, baby. I'm gonna getcha."

Dropping to his knees, Asher slid an arm under me, taking some of the pressure off of my chest. I drew in a breath, the first full one I'd been able to take since the crash. The influx of oxygen was heavenly.

As I had done, Asher pushed the seatbelt's release button then pushed it again. He turned his face toward mine. At this angle, our noses practically touched and his eyes were a bit out of focus. Beads of sweat covered his forehead.

"I'm gonna have to get something to cut this with, okay? I'll be right back. You hang in there."

"Ha ha."

He smiled at me. "That wasn't meant to be a joke, but I'm glad to see your sense of humor didn't suffer any damage." His eyes scanned me quickly. "Anything else hurting?"

I shook my head, jostling what felt like the entire volume of my body's blood content. "No. I'm just shaken up. And it's a little hard to breathe."

The creases came back to his face. "Okay. I'll be right back."

"Don't take too long, okay?" The words were an anxious whine.

"I won't. I promise. You can time me if you want."

He withdrew from the car, and I watched as he got to his feet, watched his boots retreating. Because I had nothing better to do and I was starting to feel a bit claustrophobic and panicky, I did count. "One, two, three, four…"

By the time I got to twenty, Asher's boots were back in sight. At twenty-five, he was once again crowded into the squashed front seat with me, this time holding an open pocketknife.

"How'd I do?" he asked as he slid the knife under the seatbelt near the clasp and began moving his hand in a sawing motion. His other arm was beneath me again, I supposed ready to catch me when the belt was severed. I could hear his rhythmic breathing as he worked.

"Twenty-five seconds. Not bad."

He grinned and shook his head then paused in his sawing motion. "You know, before I finish up this heroic rescue, I've got to say something."

I furrowed my brow. "What?"

"Well, correct me if I'm wrong, but… I do believe you're having a problem."

In spite of my bizarre circumstances, I laughed. Which hurt my ribs. "Maybe," I conceded.

"No, come on now. Admit it. You've got a problem, and as promised, I'm helping you solve it."

"Are you going to leave me hanging here all day if I don't play along?"

"Maybe." He smiled.

"Then yes, Asher, I have a problem. Now would you please get me the hell—"

Before I could finish the sentence, he made the last cut and sort of dived beneath me so when I dropped the short distance from the belt, I fell onto him and not the car's roof or the shattered windshield. For a second we lay there, his arms wrapped tightly around me.

"I got you," he said into my hair. "I got you. You're okay now."

I allowed myself to soften against his chest and breathe deeply. He smelled like freshly cut grass and yummy guy shampoo and smoke. Oh yeah, the fire. I lifted my head and looked around.

"We should move—"

"It's okay," he said. "The fire's across the street—the factory. You lie still. I'm going to slide out and bring you with me, in case you've got a broken bone or something and don't realize it yet. You may be in shock. Just pretend I'm a stretcher."

I nodded and clung to him, feeling my pulse recede and wondering for the first time why a teenaged boy was performing my rescue instead of a firefighter or someone more qualified, someone with an actual stretcher for instance. Not that I was complaining—I couldn't let human paramedics examine me anyway.

And then we were free of the wreckage, and I understood.

The scene outside the car was utter pandemonium. Gingerly, I got to my feet, taking inventory of my own body before looking around. The beautiful church I'd been admiring was blackened on one side, those multi-colored windows in jagged pieces or missing altogether. Across the street, a low, stretched-out building was fully engulfed in flames. It looked like a factory or a one-story warehouse.

Several other wrecked cars were scattered on the street, in various stages of annihilation. Mine hadn't gotten the worst of it. Or the best.

I turned to look at the wreckage of my little convertible and all the air deserted my lungs at once, leaving me struggling for breath once again. It was smashed. How had I even survived it? Feeling dizzy, I rocked on my feet.

Asher's arms came around me again. "You okay? You should sit down until the EMT's can take a look at you." He walked me to the nearest curb and guided me to sit, his supportive arm still around my back.

"What happened?" I finally thought to ask the obvious question.

"I'm not sure. That's the Magnolia Sugar Tea Company. I was down the road near the park when I saw the blast. I drove up as close as I could and got out to see if anyone needed help, and then I saw your car. That's as much as I know."

I stared at the flames, the black smoke pouring from the open roof of the building. The heat of it was immense, even here across the street. It was hard to look at it without squinting.

"Do you think anyone was inside?" If they had been, it was unlikely they'd survived.

He shook his head. "No. I don't think so. It's closed for the night. My buddy's checking inside the church." Lifting his eyes, he scanned the fiery scene. "Oh man, Ryann's gonna be torn up. Her grandma, too." He turned back to me. "She's one of my classmates. It's her family's business."

A cold sensation seized my heart. Ryann's tea factory. *Culley's mission.* Was that what he'd been talking about? Had he been sent here to take out the source of the tea that was freeing humans from Elven influence? I twisted away from Asher and dry-heaved over the sidewalk.

His hands came to the back of my head, sweeping my hair back from my face. After waiting for my spasm to pass, he said, "I'm gonna see if I can get somebody to check on you. They've got their hands pretty full, though. God this is a mess. You'll be okay here for a minute?"

I nodded weakly, but I was *not* okay. How could Culley have done this? I didn't know him well, but after spending the past week or so with him, I didn't think he had this kind of evil in him. Yes, he'd advised me to simply do my job, not to "think about whether it was right or wrong." He said that was what he always did. But this was so extreme. He might have killed people tonight.

Asher hustled toward a nearby ambulance, where uniformed paramedics were loading a writhing man into the back. I glanced around again. It seemed like everywhere

I looked there were shocked faces, some people crying, others running toward the destruction or away from it. A mother shielded her young child's eyes from a pool of blood in the street near another one of the ruined cars.

Within two minutes Asher was back, kneeling in front of me. With a hand under my chin, he tipped my face up so our gazes met. Those incredible turquoise eyes were so serious, so full of concern.

"Listen, they know you're here, and they're going to get to you as soon as they can. There are a lot of people who need help—a lot of people hurt. I need to help out—there aren't enough emergency personnel to handle it all. You stay right here, okay? Don't get up and wander off. You need someone to check you out. I'll be back for you as soon as I can."

I nodded, but he wasn't satisfied.

"Promise me Ava. Don't leave before I come back."

"Okay. I promise." It wasn't a hard vow to make. I had no way to leave. My car was a lopsided pancake in the middle of the road. I didn't feel like moving anyway. I was sort of numb and disconnected. This was horrible. And I felt responsible, like I should have prevented it or something.

Maybe it had been an accident? My spirit lifted for a second then immediately sank again. Not likely. It was too coincidental that Ryann's factory had blown up the night after Culley left Altum. He must not have headed for L.A. right away as he'd said he would.

I'd been wondering how he planned to get home anyway. I had picked him up from the airport in Memphis last week after driving cross-country myself. He'd had a modeling gig in New York City and couldn't drive out with me from the west coast—not that I'd *wanted* to share a three-day car trip with him. Now I was hoping I never saw his face again.

From somewhere behind me I heard the screech of car tires. Another town resident getting a first look at the carnage, no doubt. At the sound of footsteps hitting the pavement at a dead run, I turned at the waist to look. I'm not sure why. I guess that's just what you do when you hear someone running toward you.

It was Culley. *Great.* I got to my feet, now feeling stiff and sore all over, prepared to walk away from the devil approaching me with his designer clothes and tense expression and treacherous beauty.

With his unnaturally good looks and tall, athletic physique, he resembled an actor on the set of an action movie more than a real person happening upon a real disaster scene. Of course he *wasn't* a person, not in the literal sense of the word.

When he spotted me, Culley's pace slowed to a saunter. And I didn't walk away. No, I wanted to confront him, make him account for what he'd done.

By the time he reached me, his face had lost all traces of concern and displayed his typical nonchalance. His eyes roamed over me, assessing, perhaps checking to see whether his plot against the humans would lead to any unfortunate collateral damage. Then his gaze slid to the side, taking in my destroyed car, and back to me.

"Good thing you dumped me, Angel. If I'd been in that passenger seat, the world would be minus one Culley Rune."

"Yes, that would have been tragic," I deadpanned. "What are you doing here, Culley? I thought you'd be long gone by now."

"I was. I made it to the airport in Memphis."

"But then you decided to come back to the scene of the crime. I guess criminals do that sort of thing—I've seen it on cop shows."

His eyes flared. "Criminals? You think I had something to do with this?"

"Didn't you? Wasn't this your mission?"

For a moment, I thought I saw a glimpse of hurt in his eyes, or insult, but then it was gone, replaced by flinty blue obstinance. "I did not. It was not." He reached toward me, laying a hand on my arm. "So, you're okay? You're not hurt?"

I shrugged away from him. "No. I'm fine. I was lucky. Which is more than I can say for a lot of people here tonight."

Across the street, someone yelled for help, and a couple of girls Asher's age ran toward him. Culley didn't even turn his head. He was still focused on me.

"And what about back at Altum with the Light King? And Nox? They didn't punish you? Or did they just throw you out?"

I shook my head. "They did neither. Listen, I don't really have anything left to say to you, okay? You've verified that your bomb worked, or whatever, so you should probably get back on the road."

Now Culley's eyes narrowed. "I didn't do this, Ava. I've already told you that. Do you really believe I'm a... a terrorist?"

The word *no* leapt to my mind, but what other explanation was there? Why else would he have come back here? "I believe you do what your father commands you to do. And I know you're good at making people see what they want to see."

I'd discovered Culley's unique glamour on the day I'd met him—we'd been on a shoot together, and it quickly became obvious why he was the world's most in-demand male model. He wasn't *just* attractive. He'd explained it fell along the lines of the old adage "beauty is in the eyes of the beholder." No matter who was looking at him, male or female, child or adult, human or Elven, they all saw their ideal—he was literally the best-looking guy they'd ever seen.

Culley smirked. "Believe it or not, Ava, my glamour and my moral center are two separate things. I'd think *you* would understand that, if anyone would."

Ouch. The comment jabbed my insides and left a stinging gash. But he was right. For years, I had used my own glamour to hurt people in service of Culley's father Audun, the head of the Dark Council. I'd erased their memories or implanted new ones, and it had made me feel like scum. I was seriously hoping that just because a glamour

11

could be used for evil purposes, that didn't mean it *had* to be.

In fact I was making my break from the Dark Court and setting off on my own when my car had been caught up in the crossfire of this tragedy.

"It doesn't matter what I think. You should be worried about what these deputies milling around here are going to think," I said. "You're a stranger in a very small town at the wrong time. So am I. We both need to go."

Culley stared at me for a moment. Then he took my hand. "Come with me."

I yanked my fingers from his grasp as Asher walked up. His eyes went from me to Culley, back to me again, clearly taking in the unfriendly body language.

He slid an arm around my shoulders. "Everything okay here? This guy bothering you?"

Culley bristled at his words—and his familiar handling of me—straightening to his full six-foot-three height. It put him at only an inch taller than Asher.

"This *guy*..." he said, his light Australian accent suddenly more pronounced. "... is her fiancé. So you can just nick off, farm boy."

Asher's hand on my shoulder tensed. "I wasn't speaking to you." Turning to look directly into my eyes, he asked again, his words gentle and low, meant only for me. "Are you all right, Ava?"

My heart pulsed hard, a sweet pain that tightened my throat. "He's not my fiancé." I wasn't sure why it was so important to make the clarification at that moment. "He was, but he's not anymore. It's complicated."

Asher nodded. "Okay. I want you to go sit in my truck and wait for me while I check with the EMT's. I think they're about to transport some people. Did anyone get to you?"

"No, but I'm fine."

His eyebrows lowered, and his lips stretched into a thin, displeased line. "I'm driving you to the hospital, just in case. Here are my keys. Go get in—I'll be right there."

He held out his keys, expecting me to take them. Expecting me to allow him to take care of me—keep taking care of me. I couldn't do that. And I couldn't go to the hospital. Before I had the chance to tell him that, Culley spoke up.

"Listen mate, I'll take it from here. You've been all Johnny-on-the-spot and whatever—good on ya. But *I'll* look after my girl."

Asher took a step forward, insinuating his body between me and Culley. "I believe Ava's already made it clear she's not your girl anymore."

My gaze bounced between the two aggressively positioned guys, and my pulse quickened. This wouldn't do. And though I would *not* be leaving with Culley, I couldn't leave with Asher either. I couldn't go to the hospital. I couldn't allow him to get more involved in my life than he already was. The burning building on my right was a perfect example of the reason. My world was too dangerous for a human interloper. *I* was dangerous to *him*.

I touched his arm lightly. "Asher. Can I speak with you a minute?"

He glanced over his shoulder at me, then took a breath and fell back from his standoff with Culley. Together we walked a few feet away as Asher muttered, "That guy's mouth is going to break his nose one of these days… as my granddaddy would say."

"I know. I know. He's kind of full of it." Asher dipped his head to listen as I spoke to him in a low voice. "It's okay. I'll handle him. He's harmless."

He glanced to the side, where Culley stood watching us with clenched fists and a scowl. Even now he was ridiculously good-looking. What did Asher see when he looked at him? Some kind of threat, obviously.

"Harmless," he repeated, not sounding convinced. "Did he have something to do with the reason you climbed that tower the other day?"

"Um… not directly. I can't really explain. Just… don't worry about me, okay? I'll be fine. I can handle him."

Asher's big hands enveloped mine. His sincere eyes bored into mine. "You don't have to handle anything—not alone. My friend Richie owns a body shop and a tow truck. I called him to get your car out of here and find you a loaner. In the meantime, I'll take you wherever you need to go."

Culley stepped close, butting into our private conversation. "She's going to California, mate. You planning to saddle up your plow horse and take her there?"

Asher slid an acid glance over at him. "If that's what she needs," he growled.

Culley reached out and grabbed Asher's shoulder. Asher knocked his arm away. This was getting out of hand. I stepped in between them and held my arms out to either side like a boxing referee.

"Wait a minute. Asher—thank you, but no. I don't need your help. And Culley… I'm not going back to California. You know why."

His eyes narrowed in a warning look. "They'll find you, you know. Even with a head start." Slanting a glance in Asher's direction, he added, "Even with a beefed-up bodyguard. You can't win this one, Ava."

I lifted my chin, hoping he was wrong, even though I suspected he was right. "I can try. They don't own me. It's a free country."

Culley shook his head, his lips twisting in a sad smile. "Not for us, Angel. Not for us."

Chapter Two
Tightrope

I couldn't decide whether Asher's expression was baffled or offended or maybe a combination of the two as he watched us. My attention was ripped away from his face by the sight of a brand-new Mercedes speeding up to the accident scene. The dealership sticker was still on the window.

Ryann. She was driving. Lad sat in the passenger seat. My heart twisted at the horrified looks on their faces as they caught sight of the burning factory. When the car stopped, they got out and ran toward the building.

Culley must have spotted them, too because he backed away quickly. "I believe I'll go grab a cup of coffee. I'll be around—if you need me just call."

"I will never need you," I assured him, watching his retreat. He'd be back—I knew it. And he was probably right about my escape plans.

How would I evade Audun's lackeys if he sent them out to search for me? How could I even flee without a car? And how would I support myself? If I continued modeling, it would be very easy for Mother and Audun to find me. A rising tide of fear threatened to swamp me. I couldn't think about it right now. I'd figure it out later. All I knew was I needed to get away from this horrible disaster scene and from Asher's troubled gaze.

"Don't go with that guy, Ava," he said softly. "I get a bad feeling from him. I don't know what happened between you two, but I don't think you should trust him."

Letting out a weary sigh, I turned toward him, looking up into Caribbean blue eyes that had no doubt caused many a smart girl to turn stupid in his presence. "Should I trust *you*? Who I know nothing about and have talked to three times in my life, including today?"

Without hesitation, Asher responded, "Yes." He pulled me close and whispered against my ear, "You should. You should also let me do *this*."

Then he shocked me by taking my face in his hands and kissing me—soft, sweet, the kind of first kiss I'd read about but could never have imagined. Because my imagination didn't know something like this actually existed—this tingly, floaty feeling, the warmth and softness of his lips, the heavy thump of my heart that forced my lungs to work overtime and my head to spin.

"Um… Ava?"

The familiar voice jerked me back to reality. I pulled away from Asher and blinked several times, battling to

17

regain my grasp on the world around me. I felt sort of disconnected and wobbly, grateful for Asher's supportive arm around my back.

Ryann stood in front of me, Lad close by her side.

"Asher?" she said, her voice sounding even more incredulous this time.

"Hey Ryann." He stepped toward her but kept a hold on me. "I am so sorry. Did someone call you?"

She shook her head in a dazed sort of motion. "No. I… we saw the explosion and came to see what had happened. I didn't know you two… knew each other."

Now I spoke up, snapping out of my stunning-kiss high. "We met a few days ago in town. And he got me out of my car just now." I hooked a thumb toward the wreckage that had been my Corvette.

"Well…" she said, her gaze still bouncing between the two of us, trying to figure out our apparently close connection. "I guess I'd be pretty grateful, too. I'm glad you're okay."

"Do you know if anyone was hurt?" Lad asked Asher.

"A few people were transported to the hospital—they were also in their cars during the blast. I don't know if anyone was in the church."

Both guys looked toward the damaged building.

"Do you know who did it?" Ryann asked me. Her voice was quiet, deadly serious.

"Do you mean… are you asking if *I* did it?" Cold pain cramped my insides. Did she really think I was capable of such an atrocity?

I noticed Asher's eyes slide to the side, back toward me. He'd obviously heard the odd question.

"No—of course not," Ryann said. "I'm asking if you saw anything… or anyone."

Culley, she added silently.

I answered her without speaking. *I saw him. He denies it. I don't know.*

Asher squeezed my hand. "Richie just showed up. Listen, I'm gonna go talk to him and see if he found you a rental. I'll be right back. You should get anything you might need out of your car before he scrapes it up and takes it to the junk yard, okay?"

I nodded and watched him walking toward the large tow truck that was coming toward us, carefully weaving between the disabled vehicles on Main Street.

Following his suggestion, I went to my car and got down on my knees to peer inside through the open driver's side door. The back seat was less squashed than the front. Reaching an arm into the open space, I was able to snag the handle of my overnight bag and drag it out. My suitcase was in the trunk. No way I'd be able to retrieve it until the vehicle was flipped right-side-up again.

At least my purse was there, though it was nearly empty. It had been tossed pretty thoroughly during the wreck. On my hands and knees I crawled further into the car and gathered my lip gloss, brush, gum, and some loose change. But where were my wallet and phone? *Uh oh.* I wanted to find my phone of course, but I *needed* my wallet. It contained all my money and credit cards, my driver's license, and other identification. I couldn't rent a car, buy a plane or a train ticket without it.

After a thorough search of the interior, I determined the missing items must have been thrown from the car, so I walked around the perimeter of the crash site searching for them.

"Can I help?" Lad said.

I looked up, spotting Ryann behind him talking to a sheriff's deputy.

"Maybe. I can't find my wallet or my phone. Maybe someone picked them up already and turned them in to the police."

"You should ask," he said and nodded toward Ryann and the officer. "I'm going to hang back here. I'm not exactly a registered resident of the county."

"Yeah, okay."

Taking his suggestion, I approached the officer and asked if anyone had turned in a stray wallet and phone.

"Not that I know of. Are you okay, ma'am? Were you in the explosion?"

"No. I mean, yes, my car was overturned, but I'm fine."

"Well, you better get yourself checked out just in case." He was already reaching to tap the radio clipped to his collar, no doubt to notify emergency services they had another potential patient.

I darted my eyes at Ryann. *Help me out here... please.*

She touched the officer's hand holding the communications device. "Officer Jefferson—that won't be necessary. Ava is my friend. I'll make sure she goes to a clinic and gets checked out, okay? And would you ask the dispatcher to check on that missing wallet and phone? See if anyone's turned them in?"

She was swaying him, and I appreciated it.

The man immediately spoke into his radio. "Hey Mary Lou? This is Marc. I'm out at the scene right now. We got someone who had a wallet and cell phone go missing from their car. Anybody turn anything in there?"

A static-y voice came back and informed him that no wallet or phone had been brought to the sheriff's department. He let go of the device and turned his eyes to me. "Not yet, but check back in later in the day. And give the car another look. They're probably in there somewhere. I doubt anybody around here would steal things from a wrecked car in the middle of Main Street. And make sure you *do* go by and get yourself checked out, young lady."

"Thank you, I will," I lied.

By the time I'd made one more fruitless search of the car, Nox and Vancia had arrived. They now stood with Lad and Ryann, the four of them looking like they were ready for a magazine spread. Good thing Ryann had already swayed the officer into moving along to other business—a group like them would definitely draw attention—and unwanted questions.

"Any luck?" Ryann asked.

I shook my head.

Nox and Vancia both wore troubled looks. "You're okay?" he said.

"Yes. Thanks. And no—I don't know who did it. Culley denies it."

"Do you believe him?" Vancia asked.

"I'm not sure. He's hard to read. I'm starting to think the appearance-morphing may be only part of his glamour."

"What do you mean? What is Audun's glamour?" Vancia turned to Nox. "Davis never told me. Do you know?"

He shook his head. "I'm not sure," he said. "It's not the appearance thing—Culley got that from his mom's side. Audun told me it was persuasion, something like Davis's, but I've barely spent any time with him—I've been back in the Dark Court such a short amount of time. What is it really?"

Before I could answer, Asher returned, stepping up beside me and resting a hand on my shoulder. He eyed my purse and bag. "Got everything?"

"My suitcase is still in the trunk—maybe I can get it after Richie lifts the car? And I couldn't find my wallet or my phone."

He kissed my temple. "Don't worry about that—you don't need any money right now. I'll take care of anything you need. So... you know Nox apparently. Who are your other friends?"

He eyed Vancia and Lad—and his former schoolmate Nox—in exactly the way you'd expect a human encountering three incredibly beautiful Elves to do.

"Oh, guys, this is my friend Asher. Asher, this is Vancia. She's also from… California. And this is Lad. He's Ryann's—"

"Boyfriend," she interrupted before I could utter the word *husband*. "He lives in Deep River, but he's homeschooled."

Asher sized them up for a moment and extended a hand, shaking each of theirs in turn and offering a polite, "Good to meet you." Then he shot a side-glance at me, as if measuring me against my companions and realizing we all *fit* in some strange way.

"You ready to go, Ava? We'll make a run by the hospital, and I'll get your suitcase from Richie later. He doesn't have a car available for you right now—his are all lent out. But he might be able to locate one tomorrow. For tonight— you'll stay at my house. I've already called my mom, and she said it was fine. She's making up the guest room."

As if they'd all been pinched simultaneously, my Elven friends developed shocked looks, their eyes widening.

You're staying with Asher? Ryann asked me mind-to-mind. *How well do you know him?*

No, I told her. *I'm not.* Then I turned to Asher. "Could you put my stuff in your truck? I'll be there in a minute. I need to talk to Ryann."

His glance bounced between the two of us then he nodded and picked up my overnight bag, walking away toward Big Red and giving me a few moments of privacy with my friends.

23

"I don't know how this happened," I explained to her. "But it seems like your alpha-male friend has a hero complex, and for some reason he's fixated on saving me. I'll get rid of him. Could I come back to Altum with you tonight?"

"Of course," Lad answered for her. "We'll have a lot to talk about. There's no way *that*..." he nodded toward the flaming factory. "... was an accident. We need to figure out who was behind it. If Audun gave the order he's got to be deposed immediately."

"I agree," Nox said. "But I'll find out soon enough. Vancia and I are headed for the Oxford airport from here. We'll take her plane to L.A., and I'll confront him face to face, ask him mind to mind."

"You shouldn't do that," I said. "For one thing, your safety could be in danger if you show up there and start demanding answers. There are some things going on that you're not... aware of."

"A coup?" he demanded. I could see in his eyes it was something he'd feared all along.

And here it was, the moment where I had to decide whether to switch sides completely. I felt like I was walking a tightrope suspended between my own clan and the right thing to do. On one end were these people I'd come to know as good and honorable. On the other, my heritage, my mother's expectations—and Audun's terrifying power.

I took a deep breath. "A plot, yes. To work behind your back and continue Davis's mission to re-establish Elven rule over humans. Audun... and my mother... and a few others.

They were hoping to do it quietly, without violence. They feared outright assassination would be too risky. It might turn our people away from their cause. There's been much rejoicing about your return from the 'dead,' about you taking the throne. Your parents and Vancia's were beloved, and the people want you to rule. Audun's plan was to let you be a figure-head ruler while continuing his schemes behind your back."

"I don't get it," Nox said, shaking his head, his dark brows drawn tightly together. "I mean I believe you, but he swore fealty to me. He *told* me mind to mind he was loyal to me and had no interest in furthering Davis's plans."

"Yes… well, that's the *other* thing. His glamour allows him to say something like that… while doing the exact opposite."

"He can lie mind to mind?" Vancia asked, clearly shocked.

"Yes. To anyone. About anything."

"I've never heard of anyone with that glamour before," Lad said, his grimace indicating grave concern.

"Me either," said Nox. "Well, now at least we know he can't be trusted. And he's got to be taken down." Turning to Vancia, he said, "I want you to stay here. I'll go alone. I don't want you around that pack of vipers. Who knows how many of the Dark Court he's got on his side? We can't be sure who's trustworthy."

She grabbed his hand. "No. I want to come with you."

Lad spoke up. "Neither of you should go. It's too dangerous. And barging in there demanding answers will tip off Audun that we're onto him. It could speed up his plan or even cause him to do something drastic like reconsider the assassination option. I think you should take that plane to an international airport and go abroad again— skip your California trip entirely. Go work on the international tribes and gain their trust and cooperation. It'll help to have that strength in numbers when we eventually do confront Audun and his co-conspirators."

"Do you really expect me to jet off and just let this... this cancer in the Dark Court continue to grow?" Nox said.

"Be calm, brother. You'll have your chance to do some 'surgery' within your court," Lad assured. "But you need more information first." He turned to me. "We need someone on the inside to find out how strong Audun's backing is, to find out who's with him. And to figure out his next move. He's taken out the tea production—for now. We need to know what he plans to do to re-establish Elven rule—bring back the fan pods? Use politics? Physical force?"

Now all their gazes rested on me. I started backing away, my palms up in front of me, my hammering heart rising up to block my throat.

"You don't mean... I don't think I can... I can't go back there. I *wasn't* going back there—ever. I don't want to work for him anymore. You don't know what Audun is like."

"But *you do*," Lad said. "And apparently he trusts you— he sent you here to strike a blow against the Light Court. He arranged for you to be betrothed to his son. If anyone can get close to him, you can."

"But Culley knows what I did," I argued. "… confessing to you and repairing the damage to your memory. What if he tells Audun?"

I'd never been the direct recipient of Audun's wrath, but I'd certainly heard the rumors. At times, I'd been one of his methods of punishment.

"Culley cares about you, Ava," Ryann said. "I suspect he could be very easily persuaded to keep his mouth shut, as long as he believed there was a chance you cared for him, too."

"No. I can't. There's another aspect to Audun's glamour—and if Culley *has* inherited it, he'll know what I'm up to. Audun is like a walking, breathing lie detector. He can lie to anyone, but no one can lie to him. I've seen it in action."

"And I've seen you and Culley together," Vancia said. "There *is* something there—attraction at least. We need you Ava. You're the only one who can get inside the Dark Council and tell us what's really going on. Many lives may depend upon it—human and Elven."

As she spoke the last word, her gaze drifted over to Nox. She was clearly afraid for her husband's life. As long as the Dark Council was plotting against him and against peace with the Light Elves and with humans, Nox's life would be in jeopardy.

I couldn't let the two of them go to L.A.

But I also couldn't go back there myself. I had changed. I had gotten a taste of what it was like to make my own decisions. I'd seen a glimpse of a future free from hurting

27

and using others for the gain of the Dark Council. The thought of being in Audun's presence again, under his thumb again, made my skin crawl and my belly sick with dread.

Casting a glance to the side, I saw Asher sitting in the cab of his truck, waiting patiently as I'd asked him to do. Suddenly, a ride with him in Big Red seemed very, very appealing. I wanted nothing more than to climb up into the seat beside him, turn up the radio, roll the windows down, and tell him to drive as far and as fast as possible in the opposite direction from the west coast. The Florida Keys were sounding just about perfect right now.

"I know you're afraid," Ryann said, obviously reading my emotions. "I know what it feels like to worry that your heritage and your glamour make you a bad person. I've been there. But this could be the first step toward forgiving yourself and moving ahead free and clear from guilt. Running away might sound attractive, but you can't run from yourself or your past. You have to face them."

Shaking my head and fighting tears, I whispered, "No. I can't. I'm sorry."

"Think about it. You could turn your gift into something beneficial instead of something destructive," Lad encouraged. "I've learned that myself about my leadership glamour. I couldn't run from my birthright. Instead, I adapted it to my own identity. You have a choice here. I'm asking you to help us—help the humans, like your friend Asher."

Before I even had a chance to do the natural thing and turn to look at Asher again, there was a loud cry from his direction. His voice. I recognized it though I'd never heard it that loud—or that upset—before.

"No! No. What was he doing there?" he said.

I whipped my head around to see him, now standing beside his truck, the door wide open, and a man talking to him with a hand outstretched to Asher's shoulder as if to calm him. Or comfort him.

Without a word to my companions, I ran toward him, reaching his side in moments. "Are you okay? What's wrong? What happened?"

Asher's face, which had been so appealingly tan before, was now whitewashed with shock. He turned his dazed eyes to me. "It's Granddaddy. He was in the church. They took him to the hospital and then transferred him to Oxford— he's in the intensive care."

"Oh no," I wheezed, finding it hard to breathe. I didn't know Asher well, but I knew his granddaddy was extremely important to him. This put a very real face on the tragedy. It wasn't just the destruction of Ryann's factory and the important product being made there.

It wasn't just "humans" who'd been hurt. It was someone's loved one. Asher's loved one. It could easily have been *him* who was caught in the crossfire of the Dark Elves' plot against the humans, and that thought was nearly unbearable.

"I'm so sorry," I told him, wrapping my arms around his waist.

He covered my head with a large hand and pulled it in to his chest, crushing me against him. When that big chest began to shake and then to heave with sobs, my own heart cracked open. I buried my face against him and held him as tightly as I could, whispering over and over again, "I'm sorry. I'm so sorry."

He could never understand *how* sorry I was. My people had done this—maybe even my former fiancé. Lad and Ryann were right. I had to do something. I couldn't let Audun get away with hurting people like Asher and his family. If there was anything I could do to stop him—I had to try.

CHAPTER THREE
SOMETHING PRECIOUS

"I have to go see him." Asher's voice was hoarse with grief and worry.

"Of course." I nodded against his chest, loosening my arms and stepping back to see his tear-streaked face. God, he was beautiful. Not perfect in the way Culley was, but imperfectly, completely beautiful. And it killed me to see him like this.

Motion in the periphery caught my eye. Culley stood leaning against the rear bumper of a white Jaguar parked down the street. He looked straight at me. *Let's go Angel. It's getting a bit hot around here. There's a whole squad of state police cruisers headed this way.*

As if on cue, a loud siren wailed through the muggy evening air.

If you think I'm going anywhere with you… I let the thought end there. Even as I refused him I realized what I had to do. If I was going to go back to the Dark Council and help the Light Court, I needed a way to get there. My car was destroyed. I didn't have any identification or any money or even a phone.

Be reasonable, love, Culley said. *Based on what you said earlier about small-town police, you and I need to make ourselves scarce before the big guns arrive on the scene.*

Unaware of our silent conversation, Asher took my hand. "Come with me to the hospital?"

I looked back up into his distraught face. Then over at Culley again. Everything inside me wanted to stay with Asher. But I met his gaze—for one last time—and told him no.

"I can't. I'm so sorry. I wish I could but I have to go."

"Go? Back to California? Right now?" He glanced to the side. He obviously spotted Culley, too, because his eyes narrowed, and his jaw hardened. "With him?"

I nodded. "I know you don't understand. But I really have no choice."

The remarkable turquoise eyes seemed lighter, glistening with tears. "I wish I could take you—I know I said I'd drive you wherever you need to go. I wanted to be there for you… but… my granddaddy."

His voice broke on the last word, grabbing my heart and pulling a piece of it off for himself. How could he be apologizing to *me*? How could he even be thinking of me at all? He had his own problems now.

Anyway, the best thing I could do for Asher was get out of his life. One day, if I managed to succeed in taking down

Audun and his followers, I would know I'd helped Asher in a distant, indirect way. That would have to be enough.

I pulled away from him and started walking toward Culley, my throat tight and sore, an uncomfortable pressure building behind my eyes. *I will not cry. I will not cry.*

"Ava—wait."

I turned to see Asher closing the distance between us. Was he going to kiss me again? My heart leapt into an erratic rhythm at the thought. But no, he was holding my overnight bag in one hand and my purse in the other.

"Here." He handed them over to me. "What about your suitcase? You're not even going to wait for that?"

I shrugged. "They're just clothes." Designer clothes that had cost a fortune and would end up buried in a junkyard in rural Mississippi. It didn't matter at the moment. Not when I was leaving something far more valuable behind.

On impulse, I removed my *most* precious possession—a ring my dad had worn. It was a gold and silver band, engraved inside with Elven script. I knew Asher would never be able to read the words, but I didn't care. For some inexplicable reason, I wanted him to have it—desperately. I pushed the ring into his hand.

"This is for you."

He opened his palm and looked down at the shiny circlet, which looked impossibly small in his huge palm. "It's pretty. What is it?"

"It's just… a trinket. You saved my life. Twice. And I want to give you something… so that maybe you'll remember me—or something. I don't know." It was a mistake. I shouldn't have done it. And I shouldn't say what I was about to say—if I could even get the words out around the sob that was threatening. "I'll never forget you, Asher."

And then I turned and literally ran toward the car where Culley waited behind the wheel. Throwing my bag into the back first, I climbed into the passenger seat.

"Go," I said to Culley, and as we pulled away, I did not look back.

Not with my eyes anyway.

Chapter Four
Change of Plans

"So…" Culley began, wearing a smile that was a little too self-satisfied.

"Don't talk to me," I muttered. "I'm only here because I literally have no other choice." Staring at the landmarks of the tiny town passing outside the window, I felt as if bits of my heart were snagging on them and ripping away. Nothing in me wanted to leave here. Nothing in me wanted to go home.

Culley followed my request, refraining from conversation as the miles slipped away, and I hunkered down for the twenty-eight hour drive to Los Angeles. I was the first to break the long silence, but only because he'd missed a crucial turn near Memphis.

"You were supposed to take I-40 west toward Little Rock."

The corners of his lips lifted slightly. He kept driving, totally unbothered by the fact he'd missed the exit and we were now heading east instead of west.

Straightening from my slumped position, I looked around. "What's going on? What are you doing? Are we going to pull off for a break or something?"

Culley's eyes stayed on the road. "We can if you need one. I'm fine to keep going for a while."

I stared at his profile, ridiculously handsome and irritatingly smug. I had a bad feeling. "Culley... *where* are we going? The sign says this takes us through Nashville."

Culley nodded. "Yes. And eventually leads to New York."

"New York? We're going to the city?"

"Father decided a break from the 'heat' was in order." He glanced over at me briefly. "He knew Nox would charge off to California as soon as he got wind of the explosion. Father's instructed *us* to report to his office in Manhattan. You have a place there as well, right?"

Knocked off balance by the sudden change of plans, I responded in a distracted tone. "It's not mine—a bunch of us use it as a flop house when we're in the city for modeling jobs. I have about six roommates who rotate in and out." My mind raced, trying to figure out what this all meant. For one thing, it meant I'd be facing the Dark Council leader not in three or four days, but in two. New York was only about seventeen hours away by car.

"You talked to Audun today?" I asked.

"I did."

"And…" I waited for him to continue but he stayed frustratingly silent. "What did you tell him about me?" I needed to know whether I was about to walk into a hornet's nest or a pit of burning lava. One option would be painful. The other, deadly.

"Don't worry—I didn't inform him of your… change of heart." He smirked. "I'll leave that to you. I did have to tell him your efforts to stop the wedding and drive a wedge between the Perfect Brothers were *unsuccessful.*" Culley's eyebrow lifted. "He was not pleased."

"I bet. So… go on. I'm sure he *was* pleased when he heard how successful *your* mission was."

His expression shuttered. "We didn't really discuss it."

My arms folded across my chest as I arched one brow at him. "Right. You didn't tell him about the factory."

Now Culley's blasé tone changed, turning sharp with annoyance. "I've told you repeatedly—that wasn't me."

"Oh really? You're telling me you had nothing to do with it?" Mind to mind, I challenged him. *Admit it, Culley. You know I'm not perfect. I can hardly throw stones at you. Just be honest.*

"Speaking of honesty and past sins… what exactly *did* you do for my father that has you so morose and self-flagellating?

I glared at Culley. *Stop stalling. Did you or did you not blow up the factory?*

Pulling his gaze from the road, he aimed it directly at me and answered mind to mind. *No. I did not.* His eyes returned to the road, and he drove in silence.

Could it possibly be true? I wanted to believe him. I didn't want to believe he was capable of such wanton disregard for human life, that he was as evil as his father. But I couldn't be sure. He'd been so evasive with me, so cryptic about his mission in Altum. When we'd parted yesterday in the woods, he'd said he had "everything he needed." What did that mean? Maybe he'd actually tell me.

"Since we're being all open and honest now… what *was* your mission if not to disrupt the tea production?"

He cleared his throat, shifting in the driver's seat. "I'm not at liberty to discuss it."

Of course. Frustrated, I came back with, "Well, if you're so loyal to your father, why didn't *t* you tell him what I did?"

Culley grinned. "You'd rather I turned you in?" Shrugging his shoulders, he said, "You're my betrothed. You're so fond of the humans—don't they have some sort of law about not testifying against your better half?"

"That's not an answer, Culley."

"I have my reasons. Just as I suppose you have yours for doing what you did. Speaking of which… why are you decorating my passenger seat and not tucked away in the charming Kingdom of Mud with your new BFF's right now? What changed your mind about coming home with me? Afraid you'd miss me too much?"

"Terrified." I rolled my eyes. And now we'd reached the point where *I* couldn't be honest with *him.* I was here because I needed answers. From his father. From him. I had to find out who was behind the tea factory explosion and what else the Dark Council had up its sleeve. Returning to the Dark Court embedded with my "betrothed" was the most effective way to get it done.

I told Culley the only thing I could. "They aren't my people. There's no place for me there. At least at home I'm needed." *To help your father ruin people's lives and take over the world.* That was the part I *didn't* say. I also didn't tell him I'd be out of there as soon as I got the information I needed and secured my own transportation again. The explanation seemed to satisfy him.

"Too bad about your Corvette," he said. "I always liked that car—very sexy—it fit you."

I ignored his flirting.

"What do you think of this car?" He gestured to the posh interior of the Jaguar. "I picked it out with you in mind."

I turned to look at him, baffled once again. Why would he do that? *If* what he said was even true. "It's okay."

Culley's mouth turned sullen, and his tone soured. "I suppose *you* prefer big pickup trucks now," he said. "One has to wonder why a guy feels the need to drive something *that* large. I have a theory about vehicles and compensating for—"

I cut him off. "There's nothing going on between me and Asher, if that's what you think." The last thing I wanted was to transfer the target from my own back to Asher's. He had nothing to do with any of this—I wouldn't even be seeing him again.

Culley let out an incredulous laugh. "Right. It didn't look like 'nothing' when you were exploring the inside of his mouth with your tongue."

The air wheezed from my lungs. Culley had seen us kissing? I had thought he was out of sight distance. Or really, more correctly, I hadn't been *thinking* very much at all. I'd been so blown away by Asher's kiss I'd lost all awareness of our surroundings and who might or might not be witnessing that life-altering moment.

"That was… that was him, not me. And I stopped him."

"Yes, I could tell you detested every minute of it." Culley flicked his hand in a dismissive gesture. "No matter. Farmer Fred is back there in his natural habitat of Timbuktu, and you and I are on our way back to where we belong."

I nodded as if agreeing, but New York City, Los Angeles, Milan—the places I'd lived and worked no longer felt like where I belonged. My mind drifted back down the highway to the quaint storefronts and churches and tree-lined sidewalks of the tiny southern town that slipped further away with every passing mile.

Then it drifted to that searing, mind-scrambling kiss— and my heart clenched into a painful knot. How could I have gotten so attached so quickly? It was stupid. It was impossible. And I *would* forget Asher… somehow. Sometimes I wished I could use my glamour on myself.

Chapter Five
Tootsie's

It was a quiet ride. Painfully, mind-numbingly quiet. But once Culley and I established we didn't trust each other, small talk was impossible.

His usual charm seemed to have evaporated, and I didn't have the energy verbal sparring with him would require. We'd both have to develop some acting skills pretty damn quick if we were going to fool his father about our relationship when we arrived in New York.

Music provided some distraction. Culley's rental had satellite radio, so I shuffled through the channels, searching for something decent to fill the silent space. He reacted to none of the songs, and I didn't ask about his preferences. If he hated something, he could change it.

Scrolling through the low-number channels that played music from past decades, I caught a familiar note and turned back to the 70's. James Taylor's "Your Smiling

Face," was on—near the beginning, too, which was awesome—it was one of my all-time favorite songs.

I started to reach for the volume control, but Culley beat me to it. He turned up the song until the singer-songwriter's sweet voice filled the car.

Glancing at me briefly, he offered, "I love this song."

I broke eye contact first and stared out the windshield, letting the memories wash over me. My father, singing to me at bedtime. The more he sang about my smile, the wider my smile grew until my cheeks were sore and my heart was full. I'd drifted off to sleep in perfect peace after he sang the final notes and kissed my cheek.

"You're a fan as well, I see," Culley said when the song ended.

I let my expression drop immediately—I didn't even realize I'd been smiling. Shifting uncomfortably, I said, "Yeah. I like it. I'm surprised you know it—it's old."

He nodded. "I remember it from when I was a kid."

Without me inviting him to continue, he did. "I was twelve, I think, nearly thirteen. We were riding in the car, Mum and me, and it was hot outside—it was around Christmas—we had the windows down. She'd let me ride up front with her for the first time, and I remember being all jazzed about that. The song came on, and I was about to switch it because it was oldies crap, you know, but she started singing, like, really loud. I'd never even heard her sing before, that I could remember. I left the station on and just listened to her. She sounded so happy. So different. Her face was all lit up, and she glanced over at me watching her and laughed and then she grabbed my hand and held it while she sang. I was so shocked I let her. I remember thinking…" His voice drifted off and he stopped and shrugged.

"What?"

He hesitated, but then he finished the story. "I remember thinking… we're going to be all right. We don't need him, Mum and me. We'll be fine on our own, just the two of us." He smirked and sniffed a laugh. "That was about, oh two or three weeks before she packed me off for Eton."

The warm glaze that had gathered around my heart hearing Culley talk about his mom cracked and shattered. A dull ache replaced it. This old song reminded us both of our parents. For me it was a memory of how my dad was always there for me. For Culley… it reminded him of how his mom and dad were not.

"Why did she? Do you know?"

He darted a glance at me and then went back to watching the road ahead. "I dunno. World class education, expand my horizons, blah, blah, blah." He paused a long moment but then went on. "I always wondered if she sent me away because I was growing up—and starting to look like my father to her."

I nodded. If that was true, it was awful, but it made a twisted sort of sense—if Audun and Falene had issues, Culley's face would be a constant reminder. That was if he looked like his father to *her*. What if his own mom couldn't see him as he truly was? My heart squeezed in a short, sharp pulse. It had to be so disconcerting to know that no one could see the real you.

"Culley… what do you really look like? You know, without the glamour? What do you look like to yourself?"

He cut his eyes over to me. "Why does it matter?"

"I'm curious. I know everyone sees something different when they look at you, but you must see the truth, right?"

He was quiet for so long I thought he wasn't going to answer me. When he finally spoke, his words were cryptic as always. "You don't want to know the real me, Angel. Nobody does."

I didn't know what to say to that. Maybe he was right. Getting to know each other really didn't matter at this point. I would be in the Dark Court only as long as it took to gather the information I needed. After that— hopefully—I would escape and never see any of my "people" again. Becoming attached to Culley in any way wasn't just pointless, it was stupid. This was going to be a long ride.

* * *

It was a relief to see the Nashville signs start popping up along the highway. We'd spent the past four hours listening to music, making small, meaningless remarks about the songs now and then. I was ready for a break.

"Want to stop for a little while?"

Following an exit sign for downtown, Culley pulled off the highway. "Sure. It's late. Why don't we stop for the night?" Glancing over at me, he added, "You've had a long day."

Maybe it was the power of suggestion, but I yawned. "Okay." It had been a long day. I wanted a shower in the worst way. I was still grimy from the wreck, and my muscles were sore. I didn't think I had whiplash or anything, but my body was aware *something* out of the ordinary had happened today.

Nashville was a lot more metropolitan than I'd given it credit for. Modern buildings glistened around us in every direction as Culley navigated the city streets. In addition to charming old brick front buildings and honky tonks with neon signs, there was a gleaming convention center, massive arena, and the classic Greek revival capitol building.

When we reached an area dotted with restaurants and clubs and cute shops, he pulled into the parking garage of a large hotel, got out, and stretched. I grabbed my purse and slid out of the car. Before I could reach for it, Culley snagged my wheeled overnight bag from the back seat.

He popped the trunk and lifted his own suitcase from it. "Close that for me, would you, Angel?" he asked.

I certainly didn't mind, but something about the look on his face froze me for a second. His friendly smile was a little *too* friendly. I finally moved, slamming the trunk and then falling into step with him as we headed for the elevator.

My mind whirred with fresh anxiety. In Altum, Culley and I had stayed in a suite with adjoining bedrooms, keeping up appearances so no one doubted our betrothal story. But here, there was no reason for us to sleep in such close quarters.

The elevator dinged, and the doors closed behind us. I glanced up at him. "Separate rooms, right?"

Culley's eyes slanted down to me as one corner of his mouth lifted. "Of course. Whatever makes you comfortable."

I nodded and looked away from his mischievous gaze, staring instead at the lighted number panel. It felt like the temperature in the elevator rose by the second as we stood there side by side, not talking, not looking at each other. When the doors opened again, I burst out ahead of him and walked quickly to the front desk.

The woman behind it gave me a smile as big and sweet as her southern accent. "Good evening. Checking in?"

"Hi. Uh, yes… but we don't have reservations. Do you have two rooms available?" I asked. *Please please please*

"Let me check." Her long, manicured nails clicked across the keyboard. "Yes, we sure do. No doubles left, but I can offer you two king rooms, both on the fourth floor."

"It doesn't matter if they're on the same floor…" I started to explain, but Culley cut me off.

"That would be lovely. Thank you." He pulled a credit card from his wallet and flipped it onto the counter. "Put them both on this please."

His amused grin only served to remind me of how dependent I was on him during this trip. If I'd been traveling alone, I couldn't have even checked into a hotel without my I.D. and credit cards. Cash wasn't an option either because my ATM card also resided in that missing wallet.

Embarrassed to look like a kept woman—or a dependent child—I turned back to the woman to check her reaction. Um, yeah. She wasn't thinking about me or the credit card or anything in the world except the beautiful guy in front of her face. She stared at Culley as if mesmerized.

"I… I… um… yes. Of course. That would be…" She dragged her gaze away from him momentarily to slide his card, but her eyes kept darting up again and again to soak him in. Robotically, without even glancing at me, she placed a room key on the counter and pushed it toward me.

I let out a disgusted snort and took it, grabbing the handle of my bag and wheeling it through the posh lobby toward the elevator before Culley even got his key card. Mine had a room number written on the tiny folder holding it. No doubt Culley's would have that plus *another* number—the woman's own.

She was about twenty years older than him, but it was plain to see she'd be up for a little cougar action if he was into it. I did not look over my shoulder to find out if he was. It wasn't my business. Instead, I pushed the up button again and stalked the bank of doors to see which would open first.

When one did, I stepped inside and pressed the four button. Culley came through the doors right after me. "Eager for bed, are we love?" He grinned.

"Apparently I'm not the only one," I muttered.

He dipped his head, tilting it to the side. "Come again?"

47

"Nothing. I'm exhausted. You're going out I guess?"

He gave me a quizzical look. "Why would you think that? I've had a long day, too. And we've got a lot of driving ahead of us tomorrow. Thirteen hours to be exact. I considered going farther tonight so tomorrow wouldn't be such a drag, but I thought you might like to clean up and rest from your accident."

I blinked, surprised and pleased he'd thought of it. "Yes. I really would—thanks."

"Feel free to order room service and charge it to the room. That's what I'm going to do."

I shook my head. "It's too late to eat. I'm just going to go to bed—*after* a long soak in the tub—my back and neck have had better days."

We stepped out of the elevator and found our rooms were side by side. As I slid my card into the lock, Culley teased me. "Well, if you need a back rub or anything, you know where to find me."

I gave him a side-glance and a reluctant grin. "I'll keep that in mind. Don't wait up."

About twenty minutes into the most-appreciated bath of my life, there was a pounding at my door. I ignored it. Clearly someone had done more than their fair share of honky-tonking and had the wrong room.

The ruckus repeated, followed by a muffled shout. "Ava. Ava are you awake?"

Rolling my eyes toward my hairline I heaved a sigh. *What does he want?* I'd told him I'd be taking a bath and going straight to bed. If I *had* been asleep already, the racket he was making would have obliterated even the deepest slumber.

There was more knocking, more yelling. I rose and stood in the still-hot water, then dripped my way to the towel rack. A certain male model was going to suffer some facial lacerations for this.

The hotel was nice, but not high-end enough for those fluffy white robes you find in some. I wrapped a towel firmly around me and stomped to the door, flinging it open.

"What the hell do you want? I was in the tub."

Culley's eyes dropped and scanned down my body to my bare, wet feet and then back up to my face. "So you were," he purred.

"*What* do you want?"

"Pardon the interruption. I couldn't call you, of course, since you don't have your phone, and I needed to tell you something right away. I've spoken to my father, and he requires us to meet with some people." He paused, perusing my bare legs again. "Unfortunately, you'll have to get dressed."

I blinked. Blinked again. "*Meet* with some people? Tonight? Why?"

"He didn't explain himself—he rarely does. He just issued the order. We're going to Tootsie's. It's not far from here. Ever heard of it?"

"No. Do they have fluffy pillows and firm mattresses there?" I asked, the misery evident in my tone.

Culley chuckled. "I doubt it. But they do have some of the biggest stars in the country music industry stopping in to jam, and I hear their rooftop bar is ripper."

Dying actually sounded like an appealing alternative to getting dressed and going out right now, no matter how "ripper" the bar might be. Death would be more restful, anyway. My shoulders sagged, and I let out a long breath.

"Can't you go alone?"

"Afraid not. Father insisted we both go."

I sighed again. "Fine. I'll be ready in thirty minutes." Shutting the door, I went off to pout some more and to get dressed. All I had in my overnight bag—besides a change of underwear, thank God—was a red tank dress rolled up tightly. It was made of that t-shirt kind of material that doesn't wrinkle. At least it was as comfortable as pajamas.

I had no idea if the casual dress would be appropriate attire for Nashville nightlife—doubtful, but what did I care? I was reporting for duty, not trying to get a record deal. When Culley knocked a half hour later I opened the door to see him freshly showered and wearing a pair of faded-just-right jeans, a black t-shirt, and a pair of boots.

"Did you actually have those in your suitcase?" I asked, eyeing the beautiful black cobra boots.

He laughed. "No. I went out a few doors down to Big Time Boots. Too much?" he asked.

I surveyed his look. It wasn't too much. He looked perfect—as always—and ready to take a stage somewhere, projecting an I'm-a-star-but-trying-to-look-casual vibe.

Reaching down and to the side, Culley stood again and produced a smaller pair of boots, holding them up between us. They were beautiful—black leather with a silver studs and a red bird and rose pattern expertly stitched into them. They appeared to be my size.

"When in Nashville," he quipped.

I glanced down at my flip-flops, the only pair of shoes I had with me. And back up at the boots. *I really shouldn't accept them.* They were obviously expensive. And he shouldn't have bought me something without asking first. But still… they were gorgeous. And smelled like new leather. And they matched my dress.

I reached out and took the boots, kicking my flip-flops to the side. "I'll pay you back," I said as I slipped them on, losing my balance and tilting to the side as I struggled with the second boot.

Culley's hand came out to steady me. "You are tired, aren't you?" He grinned. "We'll get in and out of there as quickly as possible. And I'd recommend you stay far away from their signature cocktail, The Steve Drink. You haven't eaten for hours, and as fatigued as you are, a strong chocolate milk would probably put you under the table tonight."

"Don't worry. I have zero interest in partying with 'all my rowdy friends.' Let's get this over with. Lead the way."

Our hotel was in the SoBro District, so all we had to do was walk a few blocks down Broadway to reach the clubs. Live music flowed from every open doorway, the bands visible through the windows of many of them. When we reached a lilac-colored brick building, Culley stopped walking.

"This is it?"

"This is it," he assured me.

The sidewalk outside Tootsie's Orchid Lounge was packed, though it wasn't even the weekend yet. It might have felt like the past day had lasted a week, but it was still only Thursday night. Apparently that was close enough to the weekend for the Nashville locals and tourists. They were out in full force in the city's hottest live music district.

"We're not going to be able to get in," I said, eying the line extending from the club's entrance. My words were still hanging there in the air as Culley stepped forward, nodded to the doorman, and pulled me through the tight doorway.

The music was loud inside, but in a good way. My boots stuck to the floor a bit as we edged our way past the small stage and through the crowd toward the well-worn bar that flanked the left side of the club's interior. The air smelled strongly of beer and cigarettes though I didn't see anyone smoking.

Every inch of space on the walls around us was adorned with signed photos of country music stars past and current. As we made our way through the smiling, head-bobbing masses, I couldn't help but notice the women noticing Culley. Young and old, single or accompanied by a date, their eyes locked on him as if he was the last piece of chocolate on earth.

Culley didn't seem to notice. Either he was so used to the ogling he truly didn't see it or he'd practiced ignoring the never-ending female adoration. When we finally reached the bar, he lifted a hand. A bartender—female—nearly tripped in her mad dash to get to him and take his order. The music was too loud for me to overhear their conversation.

"What did you get for me?" I shouted to be heard over the music.

"Chocolate milk," he said. Then, grinning, he amended it. "A soda. That okay?"

I nodded and settled back to watch the band on stage. It wasn't one I'd heard of, but then I wasn't a huge country fan. They were good, though—incredibly good. The other club patrons seemed to agree, whooping and clapping at the closing notes of each song.

"So… when are they getting here?" I asked Culley, scanning the crowd for anyone who looked like they might be associated with Audun—no one here seemed to have horns. It was after midnight. The bar stayed open until two-forty-five, but I had no intention of shutting the place down.

He leaned down and said into my ear. "My contact should be here any minute. *Yours* has just arrived."

Chapter Six
Shots Fired

Culley pointed toward the stage where a handsome twenty-something guy in a faded red tee and baseball cap was making his way to the stage, guitar in hand. The musician waited until the band that had been playing stepped down from the tiny platform then hopped up and spoke close to the microphone.

"Good evenin'. I'm Trey."

There was a roar of approval, complete with whistles and drunken screams. Even I knew that name and face. Trey Copley had performed on the most recent Grammy broadcast. His new song was a crossover hit on country and pop stations, and he'd made People magazine's list of sexiest men this year. He was human—no doubt about that—but he was very attractive in a hot country boy kind of way that reminded me of Asher. The thought of him gave me a sharp, sweet pang in my chest.

"What do you mean *my* contact?" I asked Culley, but Trey started singing before he could answer me.

A tall guy stepped through the front door, coming straight toward us. He *was* Elven. Though he wore a plaid shirt and jeans with a large belt buckle, he stood out from the crowd like a racehorse in a pen full of mules. As he and Culley greeted one another, he shot a quick glance over at me and smiled.

I smiled back, hiding the shudder that went through me. Culley leaned close to my ear and said, "Be right back, love," before moving off to speak with the man privately.

I watched Trey play and sing, but my gaze kept drifting to the side where Culley and his contact conversed. Finally, the man left, but not before Culley pulled something from his pocket and handed it to him.

He came back to me and reclaimed his spot at the bar. "What do you think?" he asked, nodding toward the performer. "Beaut, huh?"

I didn't answer him. "What was that all about? Who was that guy?"

Culley's shoulders lifted and fell. "An associate of my father's."

"What did you give him?"

His eyes narrowed as he realized I'd been watching the transaction. "Nothing for you to worry about." Pulling his phone from his pocket, he handed it to me. "Father would like a quick word with you. Take it upstairs so you can hear. I'll be up in a minute with music-boy here." Culley gestured toward a staircase.

I took the phone, my belly sinking to the heels of my new boots as I moved away from Culley and up the staircase to the second level where another act was playing—two girls with guitars singing in harmony. It was not much quieter, so I took a set of scarred stairs to the third level. The purple painted walls of the stairwell were covered with what had to be decades-worth of signatures, messages, and graffiti. I had a sudden urge to scribble "Ava was here," or something like that, but then, depending on what I was here to do, maybe I wouldn't want to leave any tracks.

When I reached the top level, yet another band was playing loudly at the back of the room—a Bon Jovi cover— with fiddles—so I stepped out onto the connected open-air roof deck where the sound was more muffled then pressed the button to place the call to Audun. I hadn't spoken to him at all since leaving L.A. He wasn't a fan of talking on the phone—I suspected his glamour didn't work as well as it did in person—so this *must* have been important to him.

He answered on the first ring. "Ava my dear. How are you? My son tells me you met with an unfortunate accident in Mississippi. Are you all right?"

The false concern in his voice sickened me. If I *hadn't* been all right, it would have been his fault—his and whichever minion he'd sent to do demolition duty on the tea factory.

"I'm fine."

"Glad to hear it. Wonderful. Well, since you're feeling well and you happen to be in town, I'd like for you to have a chat with one of my clients—Trey Copley is there now, isn't he?"

"Yes," I said woodenly. This was going to be bad, I knew it. There was only one reason Audun would want me to chat with someone. He wanted me to alter Trey's memories. Which ones I wondered? Was it money, power, or sex this time—or all three? Those were the currencies Audun most frequently dealt in. What had poor Trey done? What would he be forced to do?

"I want you two to discuss his contract. Trey is my client, and it seems he's being hard-headed when it comes to some of the terms of his agreement with his label."

Of course. Trey had signed a deal with the devil. Most of the major record labels were owned and controlled by Dark Elves. There's no way they'd ever sign a human performer unless the terms of the agreement were to their distinct advantage. Like my father, Audun was an entertainment attorney. In fact, my dad had worked for him until his untimely death when I was seven.

"What do you want him to forget?"

"I need you to make sure he's agreeable to signing the new addendum giving the label lifetime rights to all his original songs as well as his name and image."

Closing my eyes, I pressed my lips together and inhaled deeply. It never got any easier—screwing people over at Audun's command. Didn't he have enough money and influence already? When would it ever end? This was *exactly* what I'd been trying to run away from.

I hated it but I didn't dare refuse him. I couldn't tip him off that I was no longer loyal to him—not yet. I had to get close to him first, keep his trust so he'd slip and clue me into his plans.

"Okay. Anything else?"

"Yes… how are things going with you and Culley?"

A chilly finger of dread trailed down the back of my neck, raising goose bumps. Why would he ask me that?

"Fine. I mean, we're good." Hopefully I was right about Audun's glamour not working well long-distance. Culley and I were far from "good." Reluctant tolerance was about the best I could honestly claim.

There was a stretch of silence over the phone then Audun said, "Excellent. We'll want to set a date for your wedding when you arrive in New York. There's much planning to do."

I had to work hard to keep from gasping into the mouthpiece. "Yes… that's fine. I've got to go. Culley and Trey are coming. I'll… see you when we get there."

I ended the call just as the two tall, handsome men reached me. Culley smiled broadly.

"Ava, I'd like you to meet Trey Copley. Trey, this is my friend Ava. She really admires your music. I'll get us a round of drinks."

Culley headed for the third level bar, and I shook Trey's hand, working to speak around the giant lump in my throat left over from my conversation with Audun. I was never going to be free of him and his demands. If he forced me to marry Culley before I could get the information I needed,

I'd be trapped forever in the sticky web of the Dark Council.

"Hi. Good performance," I managed.

Trey grinned, revealing a star-making smile. No doubt he assumed I was star-*struck* into being speechless. "Thanks. You could hear it all the way up here, huh?" he teased.

"Oh, uh… no. I… was down there at the start of your song, but I had to take a phone call…"

His grin widened. "Just joshin' with you." His eyes scanned my body-hugging red dress and matching boots, but not in an icky way. It was more of a straightforward I'm-a-guy-and-you're-a-girl kind of assessment. "So, you from around here?" he said. "You an actress? I've done a little bit of acting."

"No. I'm from L.A. …and Manhattan, but I've never done any acting." The conversation couldn't have been more awkward. What had Culley told Trey to get him up here? He was cute, but if I hadn't been given specific orders to do so, I would have had no interest in talking to him. It was time to cut to the chase. "I want to ask you some questions."

His brows pulled together in confusion. "Are you a reporter?"

"Something like that." I gestured for him to follow me to a high top table near the deck railing. Below, the street hummed with traffic and boot-wearing tourists swarming the sidewalks.

"So, what's it like working with the legendary producers at Opacity Records?" I asked once we'd settled into our seats.

Trey's expression changed immediately. He shifted into official PR mode, his speech rehearsed and formal. "I feel lucky to have the opportunity to work with the same professionals who've launched the careers of some of my favorite musicians. Do you want to record this… or write it down?"

Culley returned before I could answer, balancing three shots in one hand and a huge mug of beer in the other. He winked at me. *I know you don't want this… I just want to loosen him up for you. Pretend to sip it or something.*

"I didn't know which you'd want mate, so I got both." He slid the mug and a shot glass toward Trey before placing my shot in front of me and downing his own.

"Oh, thanks man. I don't drink the hard stuff, but this is great." Trey lifted the mug and took a drink. "So where were we?"

"You were telling me about your new deal with Opacity Records."

"Oh, um… I'm not sure what else I can say except that I'm real grateful—"

Reaching out to grasp Trey's hand, I cut him off and exerted my Sway. "I know you have some reservations about the new contract addendum."

"Wha—how did you…" he spluttered.

"You will forget any concerns you have and sign the contract as is," I said, imbuing the words with the power of my glamour.

"Sign the contract," Trey repeated, his formerly rich voice sounding dull and empty.

As it always did when I used my special "gift," my belly wrenched with a sick feeling. From the corner of my eye, I caught the gleam of Culley's smile. Did he think this was funny? I turned to look at him. No—he looked… proud. Did he *admire* me for my ability to destroy people?

I frowned at him and returned my attention to Trey. "You'll be happy with the contract changes and feel relief instead of resentment over the restrictions." Then, feeling bad for him, I added, "The music is what's important to you, right? The fact that audiences are able to discover you and enjoy what you've created. Money doesn't buy happiness." *I should know.*

My family used to have a huge income, and I couldn't remember a time when my mother was satisfied—even before my father was killed. Poor Trey. He'd never get the chance to find out if money bought happiness because he'd be a virtual slave to his record label unless he decided to change his name and go out on his own, starting over again from nothing.

Trey nodded. "Right. It's all about the music."

"Okay then. Well, thanks for the interview. Our readers will love the chance to get to know more about you."

I stood and offered Trey a handshake.

Blinking and coming out of it, he rose to his feet as well. "Yeah. It was… fun. Nice to meet you. You'll send me a copy of the article?"

"Oh sure," I said. "As soon as it's done. Hey, sounds like they're calling for an encore down there."

Sure enough, chants of "Trey, Trey, Trey," could be heard rising from the first floor along with the unmistakable sound of stomping boots.

Trey smiled, tipped his hat to me, and shook Culley's hand before heading for the staircase with his guitar. Before taking the first step he looked back toward us. "Thanks a lot. It was real good meeting you folks." And then he was out of sight.

I sat back in my chair, letting out a long breath. I couldn't release the self-loathing as easily. On a sudden impulse, I picked up the shot glass in front of me and downed its contents in one quick gulp. And then I was breathing fire. I coughed and gasped until I could inhale normally again.

Culley burst into a fit of laughter. "First shot, huh? Well, you deserve it—good job, love. Now we can go back to the hotel and get you into that nice soft bed you're craving." He stood and waited for me to join him.

I did not. Instead, I picked up the shot glass next to Trey's unfinished beer and emptied that as well.

Culley rushed over to me and patted my back as I coughed again. "Whoa there, cowgirl. Let's tap the brakes on the whiskey or you're gonna be hurting in the morning.

We've got a long drive still ahead of us. Come on now. There you go—on your feet. Let's go home."

I was on my feet, but I had no intention of going back to the room. Not after what I'd just done. There's no way I could sleep. I wouldn't be able to stand being alone in that quiet room with the memory of Trey's vacant eyes, his dead voice, his ruined future.

No, I needed loud music, and laughter, and a raucous crowd around me. And I needed the rest of Trey's beer.

Lifting the mug, I stood and headed for the purple stairwell with Culley close at my heels. He tried grabbing the mug from me as we descended. I twisted, holding it out of his reach.

"Ava—I don't know what's gotten into you, but I want you to give that to me—you don't want to drink it. It's not some flimsy American light beer. That's a craft beer—its alcohol content is about double the average."

I tucked the mug into my belly and kept going. "I'm not a child," I yelled over my shoulder at him. "I don't *need* a babysitter. I need…" Darting into the entrance of the second floor bar I spotted a big cowboy standing alone at the edge of the dance floor and looped my hand through his arm. "… a dance partner."

Surprised, the guy turned to see who'd grabbed him, then a big grin spread across his stubble-covered face. "Hell yeah, I'll dance with you. Come on girl."

He pushed through the crowd like a linebacker, and I followed, still cradling my beer mug. As we reached the floor, I took a long drink from it, then began moving to the music.

"Damn girl," the cowboy said, wearing a look of appreciation. "That drink's biggeran' you are."

"I can handle myself," I told him then took another large swallow of the malty liquid.

"I can see that," he said and placed his hands on my waist as I danced in front of him.

He wasn't a bad dancer. It didn't matter. He was here and willing. I was here, and now I definitely planned on shutting the place down. Maybe there was somewhere downtown that stayed open even later than two-forty-five—the louder and rowdier the better.

Suddenly Culley appeared at my side. "It's time to go, Angel."

He was not dancing. He was not smiling. He was *boring*. He wouldn't help me forget.

I ignored him, but the big cowboy took notice. "You know this fella, darlin'?"

Glancing to the side, I smirked. "Not really." Which was true. It was impossible to really know Culley Rune.

I turned my back to him and kept dancing. Culley left only to reappear moments later on the dance floor directly in my line of vision with a girl. Blonde and curvy, she wore skin-tight jeans and a tiny halter-style top. She looked like Country Barbie. Like all the other women in the place, she gazed at Culley with obvious desire. She pressed her body close against him and undulated seductively. His eyes lifted from hers to meet mine with a satisfied so-there squint.

Whatever. He thought he could make me jealous? Ha. I set the mug on a table to the side of the dance floor and moved a little closer to my cowboy, placing my hands on his shoulders. "What's your name?"

"Brad. What's yours? Angel?"

I shook my head and rolled my eyes, making myself dizzy. Those shots were taking their natural course. *Goody.* "No. That's just what he calls me."

"That Australian fella your boyfriend?"

"No," I said definitively. "We're traveling together. I work for his father."

He nodded, and his big dopey grin got even bigger and dopier. "So then, maybe you'd be interested in coming back to my place later. It's not that far—it's over in the West End. It's clean," he offered.

I laughed. "Sounds tempting, but I can't." *See, I'm Elven, and if I sleep with you, we'll be bonded for eternity.* "I have to leave early in the morning. But I'll be happy to dance the night away with you."

Oh God. I was drunk. When I'd said "dance" it came out sounding like "dansh."

Brad smiled. "I guess I'll take what I can get." He spun me then slipped his arms around my waist. As we danced, he continually pulled me closer. After a few minutes, his hands began to wander.

When they slid up my ribcage and his thumbs grazed the underside of my bra, I lowered my elbows, pressing them tight to my sides. Undeterred, Brad moved his hands downward. They slipped around and rubbed my lower back. Then moved lower still.

If I'd been sober, I'd never have allowed it. But as it was, I could barely feel my body. Sensations, sights, sounds—they were all starting to take on a hazy air of unreality. I'd had alcohol before—wine, champagne, light beer. This was different. I felt like someone else—someone freer, happier, someone who didn't care anymore.

Brad rubbed a hand over my bottom then pulled back so he could see my face. His bore a wicked smile. "Are you wearing a thong?"

And then his hands were no longer on my backside or any part of me, and he was no longer in front of my face. Culley was there, standing between us with a glowering face and one hand spread on Brad's chest.

"You mate," he spat out at my randy cowboy friend. "...will never know. It's *no one's* business but mine—she's my fiancée, she's off her face with grog, and I'm taking her home. Are we gonna have a problem with that?"

Brad stepped back, raising his hands in the don't-shoot-me posture. "No man. Sorry. I didn't know she was engaged. She said she didn't know you that well."

"Yes, well, we had a little disagreement, but the party's over." Culley pulled out his wallet and extracted a wad of bills, shoving them at Brad. "Here—have a drink on me."

Brad stared down at the money in his hand, then lifted his head to watch us go. I gave him a weak wave and then tried to focus on putting one foot in front of the other as Culley pulled me along. I had no energy left to fight him over leaving the bar—simply staying upright was a monumental effort at this point.

"Come on, love. You'll feel better when you get outside in the fresh air," Culley encouraged as he steered me back to the stairwell and downstairs toward the open exit door.

We emerged from the club onto the still-populated downtown sidewalk. Music poured from the doorways of the club next door and the one across the street. A party bus powered by multiple sets of bicycle pedals rolled by, its passengers laughing and chanting something I couldn't quite understand. The Nashville night was apparently still young.

Culley guided me as we started the three-block trek back to the hotel. It wasn't easy. Tottering down the sidewalk was the equivalent of an American Ninja Warrior obstacle course in my current condition.

Passing the doorway of another club, I took in the blurred picture of a small group of people leaning against its brick-fronted exterior, laughing and smoking. When I walked through a particularly potent tendril of cigarette smoke, my stomach suddenly rebelled against the ridiculous quantity of alcohol I'd consumed.

Turning toward the street, I retched over the gutter. *Wonderful.* My crappy night was now complete. Thankfully, I didn't order room service back at the hotel, so there wasn't anything but liquid to throw up.

Culley waited for me to regain my composure, rubbing my back gently. He handed me a tissue, and that's when I noticed he was holding my purse. I'd forgotten I even *had* a purse.

"Thanks." I took the tissue from him and wiped my face then resumed the painfully slow walk of shame home from the club.

"Only two more blocks, Angel. Come on. You can make it—that comfy bed awaits," Culley urged as my steps slowed to a stop.

I shook my head. "No. I can't make it." I wobbled to the curb and sat down, resting my forehead on my bare knees.

Culley's hands came under my arms, pulling me to my feet again. "Believe me—you do *not* want to sit on this sidewalk."

"I'm too tired," I protested.

My whine was cut off when Culley swept my legs from beneath me and lifted me in a cradle hold against his chest.

"No," I said and shook my head, but that only made the spinning worse. I let it fall to the side against his neck and closed my eyes. "I'm shorry. I don't usually drink sho musch," I slurred.

A low laugh shook his chest. "You don't say."

The rhythm of his steps lulled me into silence. I was so tired. Sick and tired. In spite of my suspicion that the morning would bring fresh pain, it felt too good right now to slip into oblivion and forget about this long, horrific day.

Chapter Seven
The Morning After

Someone was shining a laser beam into my eyes. The red glow was painful, and the interruption to my heavy sleep most unwelcome.

Cracking my eyelids, I located the source of the torturous light. The floor-to-ceiling drapes of my hotel room were parted slightly, and the morning sun slanted through the opening directly onto my face. I attempted to get up and shut them but only made it about an inch or two off the pillow before the pain sliced through my brain, followed by an incessant throbbing that turned my stomach.

"Ohhhh," I moaned, letting my head fall back again. "Whoever invented shots should *be* shot."

A friendly male voice interjected. "I agree. Along with the twit who purchased them last night."

Jerking my head up, I spotted Culley rising from a chair beside the bed. He stretched. My sudden movement spun the room and my stomach, causing me to lean over the edge of the bed and gag. There was no trash can there, so thank goodness it was only a dry heave.

"Don't expect anything to come up, love," Culley stated blandly. "I believe you've expelled the entire liquid makeup of your body in the past eight hours." He crossed the room and placed an open water bottle on the bedside table. "Here you go... when you're ready."

"Oh no," I groaned and collapsed back into the mattress. "What time is it?"

"Eleven o'clock. I gave up on an early start to our trip at around five a.m."

I cracked an eyelid to look at him. "What are you doing in my room?"

He grinned. "This is my room. And I brought you here because you were too sick to be left alone." As I rolled my head to the side to inspect the other half of the king bed, Culley answered my next question before I could ask it. "And no—I did not sleep with you. For one thing, you're not as *attractive* as you might imagine when you're full as a boot. For another, you needed someone to watch over you—people in your condition have been known to asphyxiate themselves during the night."

"You've been awake all night?"

He nodded.

I ran my hands over my sore diaphragm and belly. How many times had I vomited during the night? Then I noticed the fabric under my fingertips. It didn't feel like the dress I'd worn to the nightclub. I pulled it up a bit so I could check it out. Not red. A heathered gray. It felt soft. It felt expensive.

"Is this your t-shirt?" I asked.

"It is indeed."

Struggling to sit up and support myself on my elbows, I leveled a glare at Culley. "You took my clothes off?"

He laughed. "I did. And again, it wasn't *quite* the pleasure I'd expected when I've imagined that scenario in the past." Reading my perturbed expression, he explained. "Sadly, your dress was ruined. I threw it out, got you into the shower and lent you a shirt. So shoot me."

"Don't tempt me," I muttered, humiliated that Culley had seen me in such a state. Had seen me naked. And that I could remember nothing about it. I'd finally found something that could replicate my brand of glamour—getting blind, stinking drunk.

Did my victims experience hangovers like this? If so, I was getting no more than what I deserved. I'd earned this and more for what I'd done to Trey last night. *Last night.* The club. The dancing.

"What happened to Brad?" I asked.

"What do you mean—did I drop his big country arse for feeling you up? No. I left him to work his *magic* on some other overserved girl. Were you sorry to leave him?"

Culley's tone surprised me. He sounded annoyed. He sounded jealous. *Was* his interest in me more than an act? More than duty? And if so—why *me*? Everywhere we went

71

I was slapped in the face with the never-ending female admiration he inspired. He could literally have any woman on the planet. What was so special about me?

"No," I answered honestly. "I'm sorry for last night. For… all of… this."

I gestured to the borrowed shirt I wore, gestured toward the room at large. I shouldn't have even been there, much less in his bed, forcing him to spend an undoubtedly uncomfortable night in a chair—when he wasn't cleaning up after me. Ugh.

"I don't know what got into me."

"I do," he said. "You're a nice girl. You have a good heart. It hurts you to hurt others." He got up and moved toward the bathroom. "We all have our ways of drowning it out—but if I may be so bold—*you* should probably find something *other* than Jack Daniels."

Before stepping into the bathroom, Culley pulled off last night's shirt and stuffed it into the plastic laundry bag provided by the hotel. "I'm going to shower now, and then we'll get something to eat before we hit the road. As soon as you're able, you should go back to your room and pack your things."

"Okay," I breathed, nearly gasping from the sight of him shirtless. It was the second time I'd seen him that way, and the shock of it today was no less acute—the long, well-muscled arms, the wide shoulders and chest, the defined torso. Culley was a beautiful man. Even in the throes of the world's ugliest hangover, I couldn't deny it.

Closing my eyes, I sank back into the pillow, girding myself to get up. When the sound of the shower turning on came through the thin wall between the bathroom and the sleeping area, I couldn't help but imagine him dropping his jeans and stepping into the stream of water.

No. Don't think about it. It's pointless.

The vision blurred, replaced by Asher's gleaming smile, and adorable dimples, and tall, lanky form. My belly flipped—in a pleasant way this time—from the memory of our kiss. It was everything a first kiss should be, and in spite of the fact it should never have happened, I wasn't sorry it had.

I *should* have been sorry. I had no business thinking of either Asher *or* Culley in a romantic way since I'd be with neither of them. Asher was human. Culley was… Culley—and his father's son. No, I was going to be alone, and that was how it had to be.

Before I could force myself from the comfort of the bed, another set of images came into my mind. Culley—stroking my hair and touching my cheek, his voice soft and sweet, telling me I'd be okay, that I'd feel better soon and to sleep, just sleep. "I'll watch over you," he said.

Was that last night? Had it really happened or had I dreamed it in my intoxicated slumber? It was all such a whiskey-soaked blur.

My eyelids opened as I heard the water stop. Heart pounding at least as hard as my head, I slid from the bed and dashed for the hotel room door. As much as I hated to move, I did *not* want to be here when he emerged from the bathroom, wet and naked. Not after what I'd just remembered.

Not only had Culley stayed up all night guarding my sleep, I was pretty sure he'd pressed a kiss to my cheek at one point and whispered the most terrifying words I'd ever heard.

"You're mine, and I'm going to take care of you."

Chapter Eight
Secret Garden

It was after lunchtime when we finally got back on the road.

"Will your father be angry with you for getting to New York later than expected?"

"Probably." Culley turned to grin at me. "When is he ever *not* angry, though, right? We might as well *do* something to earn his lordly ire. Speaking of…"

Culley pulled to the right lane and took the next exit.

"What are we doing? We've barely been on the road a half hour."

A wicked grin lit his face. "Well, as you said, we're already late—what's a little more time? There's something I want to show you."

"Okay." I shrugged. I still felt weak, not really up to the drive and *really* not up to arguing. If Culley wanted to make a pit stop and disregard his dad's time-schedule, it was fine with me.

Entering a long, tree-lined drive, we approached an enormous brick-fronted Georgian mansion. The front of it was lined with balconies and white columns. As we pulled into the circular front drive, I read the sign.

"It's a hotel," I said in surprise.

"This is not any ordinary hotel—this is the Gaylord Opryland Hotel and Resort. After I got old enough to be 'useful' to my father, he occasionally had me come visit him here in the States. We stayed at this place once when he had business in Nashville. Wait until you see the inside."

"Um… okay," I said, the doubt evident in my tone. We'd just left a hotel. I couldn't imagine what allure another hotel could possibly hold, no matter how massive it was. Leaving the car with a valet, we walked through the rotating glass door, and I had my answer. The gleaming lobby was centered by a colorful art glass sculpture that stood taller than Culley. Looming above it, a huge inverse dome tile mosaic was set into the ceiling, bearing a striking resemblance to a giant kaleidoscope. Its pattern featured magnolias and honeybees as well as musical instruments like fiddles and banjos, a nod to the Music City.

"This is pretty," I said.

Culley gave me a knowing grin. "This is not what I wanted to show you. Be patient." Gesturing for me to follow, he bypassed the registration desks and headed for a wide open atrium area beyond them.

"So we're not checking in?" I asked.

"No. We really do have to get on the road today—but I couldn't let you leave Nashville without seeing this first."

We reached the Cascades atrium, and I was in another world. It was the closest thing in real life to Willy Wonka's Chocolate factory—minus the candy and Oompa Loompas—with indoor rivers and waterfalls, lush tropical trees and plants, and far over our heads, a glass ceiling letting in the brilliant sunshine. As we crossed a footbridge and walked the winding path, we passed bistro patio restaurants that gave the feel of dining outdoors in the fresh air while actually being inside a perfectly climate-controlled environment.

We watched dancing fountains lighted by multi-colored lights then took a passageway to another vast atrium structure called the Delta, where flat-bottomed boats took visitors for a ride on an impressive man-made river. I stood at the railing and peeked over the edge at some of the largest fish I'd ever seen in my life swimming in the waters below.

"This is amazing, Culley. It reminds me of Altum in many ways. How did humans ever build this?"

He wore a pleased expression. "Who's to say the architects weren't Elven? I knew you'd like it. You haven't even seen the best part of it yet. Come on."

He grabbed my hand to lead me toward the next indoor environment called the Conservatory, and caught up in the excitement, I did not withdraw it.

"This," Culley said grandly as we stepped onto a second-story platform, "is what I wanted to show you."

"Oh… wow." There was green as far as the eye could see. The raised platform overlooked an indoor garden that was literally several acres in size and contained no less than tens of thousands of plants. The walls surrounding it were dotted with balconies from the hotel rooms that overlooked the carefully cultivated paradise.

How lucky were those people who got to stay here, maybe with someone they loved, to explore every nook and cranny of this magical environment. I didn't have that long, but I intended to see as much of it as I could. Nothing made me happier than being near green, growing things. For the first time today, I forgot about my hangover and the rough night behind us. I nearly ran down the stairs to the main floor where a path led into the lush landscaping.

The pebbled sidewalk wound around rock structures, streams, waterfalls, and a graceful vine-covered gazebo. The air smelled fresh and alive with greenery and flowers. Each turn in the path brought me face to face with a different species of plant or flower or vine, many of which I'd never seen before. It seemed every space was filled with something beautiful. Every shade of green was represented. The plant life was complimented by spotlights in some areas and low, hidden landscaping lamps in others, giving the whole place a mysterious secret garden feel.

I turned to look at Culley at one point, unable to hold in my smile. "Do you think they'd let me live here?"

He laughed and took my hand again. "I'm afraid not, but we'll come back soon—I promise."

I was too giddy with the joy of discovery to correct him. I would come back here again someday—hopefully—but we would not be together. Still... I appreciated him introducing me to this special place more than I could say.

I stood for a moment, watching koi gliding along the bottom of a tranquil pool and inhaling the mix of fresh fragrances of the garden. My headache had calmed, my stomach settled. I felt… good. How had Culley known I'd love this? Why had he gone to the trouble of bringing me here and risking his father's ire by arriving even later in New York?

He stepped up close behind me. "I hate to say it, but we should go."

"Yeah." I nodded and turned to follow him back along the path toward the lobby.

As we stood waiting for the valet to bring our car around, I looked up at him. He glanced down to meet my gaze. A half smile curved his lips. "What?"

"How did you know? That this was the perfect place to bring me?"

He shrugged, and I could have sworn he blushed. "I pay attention. You comment all the time on plants and flowers. You mentioned starting a garden one time. I thought you'd enjoy it." He paused. "And I was right."

"Yes," I agreed. "It was wonderful. It really was the best medicine. But now we'll be so late arriving in New York. What do you think Audun will say?"

"*That* is a problem for future Culley and Ava." He nodded firmly, and his tone turned playful. "Maybe we won't even go to New York, eh? Maybe we'll turn south instead and go to Savannah—it's famous for its lovely parks and moss-strewn trees, you know. Or to the everglades of Florida? Find you some more flora and fauna to explore."

I gave him a baffled glance. Would he really defy his father completely and leave the Dark Court to travel with me? Did he long to escape it as well?

For a moment I felt a flicker of something—excitement or… hope, maybe? Maybe he wasn't as loyal to the Dark Council and his father as I'd believed. Maybe I didn't have to spend eternity alone. Culley and I could leave together, travel, see the world. We weren't best friends or anything but he wasn't as bad as I'd thought—not after the way he'd taken care of me last night and gone out of his way to please me today. We might actually have a good time together, and in time, get to know one another for real.

"Culley… what are you saying?"

He cut his eyes over at me and took a breath, opened his mouth to speak and then closed it. As he opened it again his phone rang. Culley answered.

"Yes father?"

There was a brief silence before he spoke again. "Well that will have to wait. I'm afraid we'll be delayed in getting there. Ava was quite ill last night and she's been unable to travel—we're just getting back on the road now." Another pause as he listened to Audun's response. "Of course she did her job—I'm with her, aren't I? I wouldn't *allow* her to fail."

I was instantly annoyed. His words. His self-assured tone. Scratch that thought about him ever being disloyal to Audun—he was falling in line like a well-trained soldier. He'd never defy his father even if he had the guts to. I was stupid for even thinking of us running away together. I was on my own, and that was that.

After another period of silence, Culley said in an offended tone, "Of course I did. When have I not accomplished a task you've assigned me? Don't you know me by now? It's as if I'm just another one of your subjects or something."

Before he hung up, Culley muttered, "I understand. Very well. We'll see you in a couple of days then."

He set the phone back into the console holder and drove in silence, his fingers gripping the steering wheel, his jaw working tensely.

"So… what was all that about?"

His face relaxed. "Oh nothing but our own delightful brand of family dynamics at work. And Father asked me to make a few more brief stops on our trip home."

"I see. What about Savannah?"

He glanced over at me and shook his head. "Not today, love. Maybe for our honeymoon, eh? Though I'd like to show you Australia, too."

I didn't respond to that. There would be no honeymoon for us—in Savannah or Australia or anywhere. I couldn't marry him. For one thing, I couldn't trust him. For another, as soon as I betrayed Audun, Culley would become my sworn enemy—not exactly ideal when you're bonded for eternity. No, the best thing I could do would be to keep him at a distance, keep my own plans secret, and do my best to discover what he was doing for his father.

"Where's our next stop then?" I asked.

"Washington D.C. It's about ten hours from here, so you may as well settle in—maybe you can sleep some more. It'll help you feel better."

Instead of settling in, I sat up straighter. "I feel fine now. What about you? You stayed up all night. How are you still functioning?"

"I'm fine," he insisted. "I don't need much sleep."

"Let me drive and you sleep," I said. "I'm fine with driving long distances."

"You're not on the rental form for this car."

"Oh, and now you're Mr. Rule Follower?"

He grinned in amusement. "I'll let you know if I need a break."

To my surprise, I did doze a bit during the drive. Well, more than a bit. I woke feeling stiff and sore, stunned to see complete darkness outside the car windows.

Pushing up in my seat, I asked, "What time is it? Where are we?"

"It's just after eleven. We're in Virginia. Still about two hours before we reach D.C."

"Oh my gosh. I can't believe I slept that long. How are you feeling?"

"Fine." He yawned, betraying his lie. His eyes looked bleary and heavy-lidded.

"Let me drive the rest of the way, okay? I'm all rested now."

"No. I've got it. I'm fine."

Studying Culley's weary posture and tired face, I wasn't so sure. He was probably in worse shape than I even knew because, of course, all I could see was his beautiful glamour, hiding the reality of his exhausted state, hiding the real him.

When the car weaved slightly into the breakdown lane, I decided it was time for a conversation. I had to help him stay alert or neither of us would get there alive. I wasn't in a huge hurry to reach NYC, but I also wasn't ready for my immortal life to end quite yet.

"Tell me about Australia."

His expression lifted, his eyes brightening. "It's amazing. It was a great place to grow up. Our house was near the beach, and I turned into a fish every summer, you know? I could spend all day swimming and building sand castles. Learned to surf when I was seven. I never wanted to go home—which was ace with Mum—she didn't like me underfoot," he explained. "She was always packing me off with whatever servant was nearby—when she wasn't traveling the continent for meetings and such."

It sounded like a lonely childhood to me. Most of us didn't have siblings—reproduction was a challenge for Elven couples—but it sounded like Culley had basically grown up without parents as well, raised by servants, amusing himself for hours on end.

"So you never lived with your dad then?"

His happy expression flattened out. "Not since I was a baby. I have no memories of him from back then, so it doesn't even count."

"You *do* still have them, you know. Your mind never actually lets a memory go—they're all there in your subconscious. If you'd like, I could give you back those early days when your father was around—"

He cut me off. "No." After a breath he continued. "No thank you. I've made it this far without dwelling on the 'good old days.' I think I'll hold with what I've got. I have all the *relationship* with him I need."

The way he'd sneered the word made me wonder. What *did* Culley need? Did he even know? He was so cynical and independent. He didn't seem to need anyone, but then, we all needed *someone* at some time.

"Do you miss your friends from Eton?" I asked.

"I didn't have any friends at Eton, not really. I was the only one there who was Elven. Mum and Father both warned me against letting any of my classmates get too close. The guys there—I guess they considered themselves my friends, especially when they were partying at my flat, drinking my liquor, taking advantage of all the girls who showed up because they wanted to be with me."

"Egotistical much?" I asked.

His eyes shot over to see if I was teasing, and taking in my smile, he smiled too. "I'm only telling the truth. You seem to be a fan of honesty."

"I am, actually. Go on—why couldn't you have real friends?"

"You know why. I couldn't be myself with any of them, couldn't let them know who I really was, what I was. I had some Elven friends as a child before I left for school, but it's been years since I've even talked to any of them."

"Must have been lonely."

He didn't answer. "What about you? What was your childhood like?"

"Happy. Normal, I guess. Until my father died. Then of course there was a lot of sadness. It changed my mom, made her fearful and controlling. But I had friends. I was lucky to get to grow up around a lot of kids in the Dark Court, and I also had human friends, though I never saw them outside of school."

"They weren't 'friends' then. It's impossible to have human friends."

He sounded exactly like Audun.

"You're wrong." Asher's sweet face and huge heart came to mind. He barely knew me and he'd been willing to help me, to go out of his way to take care of me. If that wasn't friendship, I didn't know what was.

Culley's gaze settled on me so long I was worried the car would leave the road.

"What are you looking at?" I asked.

"You're thinking of the farm boy, aren't you?"

"No," I lied then quickly changed the subject. "What about girls? Anyone special?"

He exhaled an exasperated breath. "I've just explained to you that I spent my entire adolescence at a boys' school."

"You must have gotten to know *some* girls—on holiday, or at those parties you mentioned."

"Depends on what you mean by 'getting to know them.'" He waggled his eyebrows in a comically lurid manner, making me slap at his arm.

"You are impossible. *Somebody* must have gotten under that thick skin of yours at some point."

He shrugged. "Maybe." And then his face tinted pink. *Intriguing.* I wondered what he had looked like to her, whomever this mysterious girl was. What was her ideal guy? Had it been his looks that had attracted her or his mischievous, hard-to-get persona? Whoever she was, I wished her luck.

"What do you really look like Culley? What's the harm in telling me?" I didn't know why I was so determined to have the answer, but this particular question troubled me. I felt like I *had* to know. "It's not like I can take a picture of the real you and spread it on the internet," I said.

"You really want to know what I look like?"

His leading tone made my pulse pick up and my heart flutter. "Yes. I really do."

"Join the club," he said, flashing a cocky grin.

Burning with frustration, I folded my arms across my chest and slouched down in my seat. "Fine. Don't tell me. Wake me when we get there."

Chapter Nine
Special Delivery

Turned out he didn't need to wake me when we reached the capital. The streetlights in my face took care of that. I blinked several times, checked the dashboard clock—one a.m. The car was parked, and Culley was not in it.

Pushing myself upright, I glanced around, searching outside the car for him. He stood in front of a faded yellow brick nightclub with another man—another Elf, I should say—off to one side of a busy ticket window.

Though it was decidedly after-hours, you couldn't tell it by the crowded sidewalk outside the club. Loud live music blasted from the open glass doors. The D.C. folks apparently enjoyed their late night revelries as much as the Nashvillians did.

I barely had time to decipher the genre of music— rock—before Culley was back in the car and pulling it out onto the street.

"What was that place?" I asked, stretching.

"9:30 Club. Good music venue."

"What were you doing there? Who was that guy?"

"Speaking to an associate of my father's." His tone was bored.

"Did you make another delivery?"

That got his attention. Culley's head whipped around so he faced me straight on. "It's none of your concern—truly." He steered to the side of the road and stopped. Away from the club, there wasn't much traffic. "Listen, I'm pretty wiped out—mind driving for a bit?"

"No. I mean sure. I can drive the rest of the way if you want."

We swapped seats, and I checked the GPS for directions back to the highway. "Where's our next stop?"

"Philadelphia. Then Atlantic City. We'll decide at that point whether to keep driving or stop and get a room."

"Rooms," I corrected.

"Right." Culley yawned and reclined the passenger seat as far as it would go. "Wake me when we hit the Philly city limit, okay?"

"Okay. Get that beauty sleep—like you need it." We both laughed. Within minutes he was out. I could tell by his slow, even breathing.

Over the next three hours I drove and thought—about the things that had happened in Altum and Deep River during the past week, about Asher, and about Culley.

Glancing to the side I took in his perfect profile, his thick platinum hair—messy from the long night—his full lips curved into a secret smile. What was he dreaming about? He was so guarded, so tight-lipped. I would never know what to believe about him.

I'd always assumed his beauty was of the skin-deep variety, that at his core he was as rotten as his black-hearted father. But he'd surprised me on this trip. Yes, he still kept secrets, but every once in a while his polished veneer cracked and I got a peek at a heart that might actually contain some softness, some goodness and generosity.

He'd been thoughtful, kind, and caring toward me. Could that attitude be expanded to include the rest of the world? Maybe even the humans someday? That would be nice, wouldn't it? I didn't want to do this alone. And I didn't want to trick him into giving me information. A partnership was much more appealing. But it was also highly unlikely. How could I ever trust him enough to include him in my plans to bring down his father? I didn't know if I could ever take the risk.

I woke him when we reached Philadelphia.

"Okay, just follow the GPS to Walnut Street. I'll jump out and run into Coda for a few minutes and then we'll be on our way."

I nodded and pulled over on the city street when we reached the address. When Culley got back into the car ten minutes later, he smelled like alcohol and perfume.

I gave him a saccharine smile. "Make some new friends in there?"

"You know how nightclubs are. And it's closing time, so a lot of the girls in there are *very* drunk and friendly." He grinned at me. "I didn't offer to give *any* of them a shower—or lend them a two hundred dollar t-shirt for a nightie, by the way."

Rolling my eyes at him, I said, "I'm so flattered. Where to next?" My finger hovered over the navigation button on the GPS.

"I'll drive now," Culley said. "Get out and switch with me."

Thanks to his mad driving pace, we reached Atlantic City in under an hour.

"It's almost four in the morning. I can't imagine what club will still be open," I said, bleary-eyed in spite of my in-car naps.

"Atlantic City never closes, Angel," he said. "Casinos, remember?"

"Ah, yes of course. So, should I wait in the car or come in? New York isn't too much further. Want to keep going?"

Pulling into a circular drive in front of one of the tall beach-front casino hotels, Culley parked it and leaned back against the headrest, exhaling a long breath. "I think it's been a long enough day already without ending it standing in front of my father. Do you agree?"

He rolled his head to the side to slant a glance at me.

I nodded. "Agreed. Let's get some sleep."

A valet opened Culley's door and took his keys while another opened mine. Allowing a bellman to retrieve our bags, we headed inside the marble and glass building. Every muscle in my body sagged with relief to be out of the car and destined for a hot bath and a pillow.

As we approached the registration desk, a spontaneous thought popped into my mind and right out of my mouth.

"It's silly to get two rooms tonight—we'll only be here a few hours—we can just share a double."

Culley glanced over at me, his eyes flaring in surprise and then narrowing. "So you trust me now, do you?"

I thought about it for a second. He'd had the perfect opportunity to take advantage of me and hadn't. Instead, he'd done everything possible to look out for my safety and comfort. I nodded. "I do."

He grinned and stepped up to speak to the woman waiting eagerly to help him.

"Checking in, sir?"

"Yes. We need two rooms please. Kings if you've got them."

My head jerked back in surprise. What was that about? Now he didn't *want* to share a room with me? If you looked up enigma in the dictionary, a picture of Culley would be there. He was impossible to understand.

After we got our keys, Culley walked me to the elevator. "Don't worry about setting an alarm. Just sleep until you're no longer tired."

I stepped onto an open elevator, liking the sound of that. Culley didn't move. "Oh, you're not coming up?" I asked.

"Not quite yet. See you in the morning, Angel. Enjoy your rest."

As the doors slowly closed, I watched Culley turn and wearily shuffle toward the casino floor, no doubt to make another one of his mysterious *deliveries*. Sighing, I leaned against the elevator's mirrored wall and closed my eyes, telling myself it didn't matter.

Whatever he was doing, it had nothing to do with me. And it was actually a good thing he'd opted for separate rooms—I wouldn't have to worry about whether I snored or how I looked when I woke up in the morning. Or what was really going on inside that thick head of his.

My only concern would be resting up in preparation for my meeting with Audun tomorrow. I'd need to be sharp. I'd need every shred of cleverness and intelligence I possessed to resist giving away my double-agency and to get out of the Dark Court alive.

I had to keep my mind on getting the information I needed to help the Light Court and the humans. The fewer distractions, the better.

Chapter Ten
Walking the Plank

I didn't know what time Culley had finally gone to bed last night or how he'd slept, but I felt like a different girl. I was rested and refreshed and ready, well as ready as I could be, to face the day.

"Good morning," he said when we met in the hallway at about two in the afternoon. "Feeling better?"

"I am. And you? Sleep well?"

"As well as I ever do. I'm starved. Let's hit up one of those overpriced buffets before we get on the road for home."

Home. "Do you consider New York home? Or does L.A. feel more like home when you come to the states?"

"Neither really. There's always a guest room available for me at Father's house in Los Angeles or his penthouse in Manhattan, but it's never the same one twice, and there's nothing of mine in either place. When I was last in the city,

I leased an apartment, but I've barely moved in there. That's where I'll be staying tonight. What about you? Want me to take you to your flat first or shall we go ahead and report to the great and mighty Audun and get that out of the way?"

Thinking of my true purpose for being here, I said, "Let's go see him. We're already a day late. Best not to test his patience any further."

"Good thinking."

I was quiet on the three-hour drive into the city, anticipating Audun's inevitable questions and mentally rehearsing answers that wouldn't tip off his internal lie detector. When I really thought about it, which I was trying my best not to do, this could very well be a suicide mission. Not only did his unique glamour allow him to lie—aloud *and* mind-to-mind—it also enabled him to determine when he was being lied *to*. Yeah, I might just be screwed here.

But I had to try—for the sake of all the humans like Asher who'd be victimized by the Dark Court if I stood idly by. Besides there *was* a chance I'd succeed. Glamours weren't infallible. Mine worked better on some people— and some Elves—than others. Audun's was most likely the same.

We were all born with our own strengths and weaknesses, natural immunities and susceptibilities. I'd never actually tried to deceive Audun before, so I had no idea whether I might be able to get away with it. Even thinking of it sent my belly swooping like a kite with a damaged tail.

My best strategy was to be as honest as possible with him without actually giving away any critical information. If he found out Lad and the Light Court were onto him and that Nox knew of his attempt to disrupt his rule and usurp the Dark Court, then my life wouldn't be the only one at risk. I had to be smart about this, starting with keeping Culley firmly on my side.

"I've never been to his New York office," I told my road trip companion.

"It's just as busy as the one in L.A." He smirked. "Plenty of celebrities needing a *good* entertainment attorney."

"Are most of his clients Elven?"

He nodded. "Most. But not all—for instance, our daft friend Trey Copley. No doubt another country artist— Elven—recommended Audun as *the* lawyer to get, and he followed blindly to his own destruction."

A sick feeling turned my stomach. Though the physical hangover was long gone, the emotional hangover from these jobs took much longer to dissipate, if they ever really did entirely. It didn't seem to bother Culley.

My face must have revealed more than I intended because he said, "About that night… why don't we just leave out the motivation for your whiskey bath, okay? If my father asks, tell him you didn't realize your alcohol limits and accidentally let yourself be overserved. It wouldn't do for him to know of your… sympathies for the enemy."

I shot him a deadly glare and he raised his fingers, keeping both thumbs hooked around the steering wheel. "I know you don't see the humans that way, but I'm afraid you're a bit outnumbered in the Dark Council. You've got to be smart. Be ruthless when it comes to protecting yourself and getting what you want. I've told you before, Angel. There's only one thing you should be looking out for—that's *you*. You've got to watch your own back, take care of your own needs. Nobody's going to do that for you, you hear me? *No one*."

My heart iced over in my chest. What was he saying? Was he including himself in that statement? Warning me against counting on him?

Culley parked in a garage beneath a glass-sided high-rise office tower, and we took an elevator to the main lobby then another up to the floor that housed Audun's offices. The ride to the top seemed to take forever. I was even more apprehensive than I had been before we'd reached the city. During our whole trip, Culley had led me to believe he was on my side. Was he going to throw me under the bus now when we stood before his father?

In any case, it was too late to back out. The elevator doors opened, and there was the name of the law firm in large tasteful letters on the opposite wall—Hade, Warwick, and Rune. I'd never met the other two partners but could only assume they were as "charming" as Audun. Turning left, we walked into a breathtaking reception area.

Spacious and bright, three sides of it housed floor to ceiling windows that looked out over Manhattan. The Empire State building was visible on one side, the Hudson River and two large bridges spanning it on the other. Low slung, expensive-looking couches and chairs were grouped here and there near the windows, and in the center of the room was a receptionist's desk.

As Culley and I walked toward her, she looked up and smiled. At him of course. *Wow.* What a knockout she was. Curling dark hair cascaded down one shoulder over a white silk blouse tucked into a black pencil skirt. Olive-skinned and sophisticated, she was like the reverse image of the flawless blonde bombshell who served as receptionist in the firm's L.A. office. She lifted the desk phone, spoke a few words, and set it down.

"Go right back," she purred. The woman gave Culley one last admiring glance and picked the phone up again, answering an incoming call.

I followed Culley, who obviously knew the way to his father's office, down a wide corridor made of distressed concrete. It had an industrial look with an upscale edge, complimented by modern art. Huge sheets of rusted metal that looked like they'd been blasted through by mortar fire or shrapnel were hung in intervals at odd angles.

The entrance to Audun's office was at the end of the hall. There was no nameplate necessary. It was unmistakably the master's quarters. The tall recessed doorway was surrounded by an ornately carved wooden frame of sorts. The double doors themselves were high and narrow, made of the darkest wood I'd ever seen. In place of knobs or handles were two interlocking halves of a large metallic plate or medallion.

Because Culley made no move to reach for them, I did, but before I could touch them the doors opened on their own, swinging apart smoothly and slowly toward us as if opened from the inside by a ghostly butler.

Culley and I darted one quick glance at each other before stepping inside.

Here we go, he said.

I nodded tightly. *Ready or not.*

In here, too, the walls were made of the same artfully pockmarked concrete. Directly in front of us was a giant abstract painting, lit by subtle picture lights. It was hard to tell what it was supposed to represent but it was dark and disturbing, calling to mind images of war but with wide slashes across the canvas that resembled a vast winding staircase.

To one side of it a small, architectural-looking settee faced an incredible wide fireplace built into the center of the wall. It was burning vigorously, lighting the room with a glow that was more eerie than comforting. There were no window walls providing generous city views in this room. It was dark and intimate, almost as if it existed on a different plane than that bright, busy lobby we'd just left.

Except for the crackle of the fire, the room was oddly silent as we approached Audun's desk. He was seated there, in a high-backed wooden chair that resembled a throne more closely than office furniture.

The desk itself was so large it could have served as a dining table. It was old and elaborately carved. On top of it there was nothing but a statuette—a strange little creature, skinny and long-nosed with gnarled limbs frozen in mid-stride, as if he'd stepped right out of a Brothers Grimm dark fairy tale. Two ancient-looking gas lamps hung suspended from the high ceiling all the way down to just over Audun's head on either side, casting shadows that emphasized his sharp cheekbones and deep-set eyes. Their pale blue was an icy glitter flashing from the shadows.

I was surprised at the interior of his office, so different from the one he kept in L.A. As "modern" as the Dark Elves claimed to be, Audun's office here looked like it had been removed from a medieval castle and transported to New York City then reassembled, piece by piece. Maybe it had. He certainly had the money and power to accomplish such a feat, and he'd had plenty of time to do it. Audun was more than four hundred years old. In fact, he'd probably had these furnishings long before New York City even existed.

Though I'd known Audun my entire life and worked closely with him many times, it felt strange to be in his presence again. Things were different. I was different.

I'd never enjoyed the things he made me do, but now I could barely tolerate the idea of working for him anymore. Our deal—the one that would have released me from his service and provided lifetime support for my mother—was no doubt null and void since I'd failed to prevent Lad and Ryann's marriage and turn the young Light and Dark Brother-Kings into enemies.

If only that factory hadn't exploded and I'd been able to keep on driving away from that tiny town, away from this bizarre life of mine. Of course that had been Audun's doing, too—it had to be. Who else would want to destroy the source of the saol-water-laced tea that had freed the humans?

Culley and I came to a stop in front of his desk, standing side by side. One of the burning logs let out a loud pop that caused me to jump. Seeing the evidence of my nerves, Audun cracked a knowing smile.

He lifted a hand and gestured. "Sit down then. And Relax. I'm not going to bite."

Crap. He was already on to me. Why couldn't I have been born with a glamour for acting instead of memory alteration? That would have come in handy right now. If Audun realized I was nervous, he'd want to know why. He'd ask questions I couldn't answer truthfully and didn't dare to lie about. I was so screwed.

"Forgive us, Father," Culley said smoothly. "We're still weary from our trip—we're not quite ourselves I'm afraid."

Audun gave him a perfunctory smile then turned to me and leaned forward over his desk, studying me. "You *are* afraid, aren't you girl? Why, I wonder? Tell me what happened in Altum. Did you glamour the Light King as directed?"

Okay, so he was going to get right to it then.

"I did," I answered honestly.

"I see. But the wedding took place anyway. And his brother, the young *Dark King*…" Here Audun rolled his eyes and snorted in disgust. "…performed the ceremony, so obviously they are still on good terms."

"Yes." My voice was small. Though he already knew the answer, I feared my response would anger him further.

"So then your mission was a complete failure."

My fingers started trembling. I shoved them under my outer thighs to hide it. In my peripheral vision I noticed Culley's head shift slightly as he took in the evidence of my nerves.

"I'm sorry. I did try," I said in a meek voice.

"What happened?" Audun demanded. "What went wrong? I've never seen your gift fail before."

And now we enter the danger zone ladies and gentlemen. What could I say? The truth would get me killed. A lie would probably have the same result. "I'm… not sure. I—"

"Apparently Lad was immune," Culley interjected. "I personally witnessed Ava using her glamour on him on several occasions. It appeared to be working—he acted quite hostile toward his half-breed fiancée, but then he appeared to rebound. Perhaps their 'love' was too strong." He smirked, showing his disdain for the whole idea of love. "My personal theory is that they'd already bonded before we even arrived."

Audun sat back in his seat and nodded, tenting his long, thin fingers in front of his chin as he considered it. "Well, I suppose we knew that was a possibility, though reports from inside the palace indicated they were maintaining separate rooms at night." He was silent a minute longer, then sat forward with new energy, once again wearing a pleasant expression.

I let out a breath, my wild pulse slowing. Maybe I would make it through this after all.

"At least *one* of you succeeded in furthering our cause," he continued, turning his pale gaze to his son. "I hear the fruits of your labors are already springing forth in Nashville and Philadelphia."

Audun pushed back from his desk and strolled across to a different set of ceiling-height double doors. They were beautiful and strange, the wood embedded top to bottom with dark stones. "I expect to hear good things from Washington and Atlantic City soon, and of course, from *this* fertile planting ground."

He pushed a button, and the doors slid apart to reveal the city skyline. Audun gestured to it grandly. "Come children, and survey your kingdom."

We obediently left our chairs and joined him at the opening. Outside was a roof terrace that held an infinity pool. If I didn't know better, I would have sworn the water ran right off the sides and down the high-rise building. Across the center of the pool was a smooth concrete walkway that led to a narrow ledge—like a plank on a pirate ship—only instead of water below there was a sea of yellow taxis on the far away city streets. There was no furniture outside, no landscaping. And no safety railing.

If I could have stayed inside the office and looked out at the sight, I would have called it beautiful—serene, even. But of course that's not what Audun had in mind.

"Join me," he said with a wicked smile and stepped out onto the walkway.

I stepped out after him with Culley behind me. It was windy on the roof, so high above the city. The magnificent view I'd admired from inside the lobby seemed too vivid here, too real. Tall buildings surrounded us, some higher than this one, some lower. Even way up here the rising sounds of the city reminded me of all the millions of human lives it held.

What had Audun been talking about? Obviously he was referring to the deliveries Culley had made during our journey. But what *were* these "fruits of his labors" he'd mentioned? Would Culley ever open up to me enough to tell me?

At the end of the walkway, Culley and I stopped, keeping a safe distance from the ledge of the building. Audun walked right up to the edge, stopped, and turned around to face us.

"Now—back to you my sweet Ava." His eyes narrowed. "What did you think of the Light Court?"

Oh God. My pulse ratcheted up again. He wasn't done with me yet—not by a long shot. No, Audun had simply decided to postpone his questioning until he got me outside, shivering on the precipice of a thirty-six story drop. What could I say that would keep me up here and alive instead of splattered down there—and was still true?

My voice quavered as I answered. "It was… interesting, very different. *They* are very different from us. They work differently, think differently."

"Your mother told me you might have been having second thoughts—sympathetic thoughts."

Ohshitohshitohshit. Thanks Mom. I drew in a shaky breath—possibly my last one. "Yes. That's true. I did for a little while. At one point I even left Altum, planning to drive away and go out on my own. But then I reconsidered and I returned—to finish what I knew I had to do." All true, though what I "had to do" wasn't exactly what he'd sent me there to do.

Audun nodded, rubbing his lips together. One of his hands wrapped around my wrist, tugging me closer to the edge with him. "Something's different about you my dear. I can't quite put my finger on it. You're giving me the right answers but… there's something you're not telling me. You do realize if I can't trust you completely, you're of no further use to me."

I stared back at him, wide-eyed, unable to control my labored breathing. This was it. This was where my life would end. The New York police and the news stations would chalk it up to just another suicide jumper in the cold, cruel city. My immortal life would come to a quick and gruesome finish after only nineteen years.

"I… I…"

And then Culley gripped my other wrist and tugged me back toward him, close to his side. He stepped forward, placing his body partially between mine and his father's.

"We've *both* kept something from you Father," he said. "We weren't sure how you'd react, and honestly, it took us both by surprise. It's all so new. It happened so quickly."

My attention was riveted to his face. What was he saying? What was he telling his father?

He swallowed, his Adam's apple traveling the length of his throat. "You see, Ava and I… we bonded while we were away on our mission."

CHAPTER ELEVEN
BOND-MATES

Somehow I managed to keep my jaw from falling open, though my heart dropped to the hard surface under my feet. And then it bounced up again to run crazy laps around my chest cavity.

What are you doing? He's going to know, I shouted at Culley mind to mind.

He ignored me and continued to lie to his father's face. "It's made her quite emotional. That's why she had some *temporary* sympathetic thoughts toward the betrothed royal couple. I take full responsibility of course. As it turns out, there is an unexpectedly strong attraction between us, and well, after all the years of abstinence, I'm afraid my patience simply ran out. I can assure you we're both completely loyal to you and ready to carry on our work—together."

He did not look down at me, but stared straight into his father's keen eyes. Blinking and fighting for breath, I turned my attention back to Audun as well. He would throw us both from the building now. Me for failing my mission and Culley for being dishonest.

But he didn't move. He stared at Culley for a long moment, glanced to my face briefly and back to his son. And then he broke into a wide smile.

"That is very good news." He laughed. "Most welcome indeed. But how foolish of you to be frightened of telling me, Ava. I know tradition holds that betrothed couples should wait until after the wedding ceremony, but it's not a custom I've ever particularly respected. It's ancient, and it's not as if it's any more likely to produce a happy lifelong bond."

His last sentence sounded like a comment on his own strained marriage. But he seemed to accept Culley's story.

"Let's go inside, shall we? The wind is picking up out here—it's not as pleasant as I'd hoped."

Clinging to Culley's hand now, I turned and gratefully followed the walkway back toward the office interior. The close, cave-like atmosphere, which had seemed foreboding before, was now a refuge. I tried hard not to sigh audibly when the big doors slid closed behind us.

Audun went back to his desk. "Well then, I'll speak to Thora about expediting this wedding ceremony. There are many dignitaries who'll want to be invited, so we can't do *too* much of a rush-up job, but we *will* want to make sure and take care of it in a timely manner, on the off-chance you're a rare good breeder, Ava. We can't have any bastard heirs to the Dark Throne running around now, can we?" He laughed so genuinely it was almost a giggle.

I managed to produce what I hoped was a passable smile. I was still in shock he'd bought Culley's story. And that Audun had just revealed openly his intention to take the Dark Throne from Nox. How else could he possibly consider Culley's future child an heir to the throne?

"If there's nothing further right now, we'd like to go back to my apartment. Ava will need to retrieve her things from her flat here and move them over. We have to set up housekeeping, don't we love?" Culley's eyes met mine, willing me to go along, and what choice did I have?

"Yes," I said. "I should call Brenna first and make sure someone's home. I lost my key in the accident along with my phone and wallet."

The two of us walked rapidly toward the door. Audun's voice stopped us before we reached it.

"Wait please."

We turned back around to face him. He was standing now. "Culley, you may go. I need Ava's services for a few more minutes… or however long it takes. I suspect it'll be an easy job for you, though, dear."

Culley's fingers tightened around mine. "Does it have to be right now, Father? Can't you see she's completely knackered from the trip?"

Audun snickered. "I'm no fool, son. I remember what it was like in those early days of bonding—and I know *why* you're in such a rush to get her back to your apartment— her *exhaustion* has nothing to do with it. Your libidos will have to wait. Your new bond-mate is my most valuable asset, and there is a client here right now. That *cannot* wait because the child's parents are in the lobby, pacing like caged animals."

"It's... a child?" I asked, stunned.

I'd worked with many "clients" at Audun's command before—in L.A. and here in New York. I'd altered the memories of men and women, movie directors, agents, senators, police officers, and other public officials. I'd even messed with the minds of celebrities like Trey to make them more pliant for whatever Audun's plot du jour was. But a child... never.

Audun crossed the floor to join us near the doors. He hit a button on the wall, and they opened silently. "Not exactly. She's fourteen—a witness in some pending litigation against one of my celebrity clients. Come with me, my dear. You'll be back with your *lover* in no time." Stepping out of the office, he strode down the hall, clearly expecting me to follow at his heels.

I'll wait for you, Culley said before we parted. His eyes were serious and filled with concern.

I shook my head. *No, go on ahead. I'll be fine.*

But you will come to my apartment later?

Raising my brows I gave him the isn't-that-obvious expression. *I don't have much choice now, do I? You've sprung the inescapable trap.*

I regretted my irritated snap almost as soon as I'd said it. Culley had just, quite literally, saved my neck. I owed him. But I was tense over having to do a job for Audun when I'd sworn I'd never work for him again. And the thought of moving in with Culley—tonight—had my nerves jangling like a wrist full of bangle bracelets. When I'd left Altum, I vowed to finally take control of my life. Now it was spinning completely out of control, and there was no telling where I would land. Right in Culley Rune's apartment apparently.

I expected to see his usual smug smirk, but instead his eyes held a shade of something I could only interpret as pain. He spun around and walked away.

See you at home—love.

I took a step after him.

"Ava!" Audun's sharp voice put a quick end to any thoughts of following Culley and apologizing. Well, I'd be seeing him soon enough.

He was my new roommate.

CHAPTER TWELVE
ASSIGNMENT

Audun's stride was long and brisk, leading me through a busy secretarial area toward a glassed-in conference room.

Inside it, a lone figure sat at one end of a shining, mile-long conference table. My assignment. A human girl who looked every one of her fourteen years—actually she looked more like a sixteen year old to me. It was sometimes hard to tell with the clothes that young girls wore and with makeup. She wore a lot of it. Short and pretty, she seemed very small in there all alone.

Audun opened the door, gesturing for me to precede him. I walked in, and he made the introductions.

"Crystal, this is my associate Ava. She's going to listen to your testimony as part of the pre-trial discovery process, and then we'll get you right back to your Saturday."

"Okay," she said in a small voice. The girl was scared, and she had a right to be. This was *not* a normal part of pre-trial discovery.

Yes, the plaintiff's lawyer or the prosecutor, if it was a criminal trial, had to share their witness list with the defense team, but the defense had no right to question one of their witnesses ahead of time, much less in a private meeting like this one.

I wondered what kind of high-powered client Audun's firm was defending. And what this girl knew about what he or she had done. Audun did not leave us alone but took a seat at the opposite end of the conference table. I sat in a chair nearest Crystal.

"So you got to take a trip into the city today. Going to do anything fun after this? Shopping maybe?" I made light conversation, attempting to soothe her obviously frayed nerves.

She glanced up at the honeycomb-like light fixture above us. "Um… maybe, I don't know. I had a track meet today, but I guess we probably won't make it back in time for me to run my events." Her gaze darted to my face. "Will this take long?"

"Not at all," I said, though I really had no idea. Obviously someone had swayed her parents to bring her here and give us unsupervised access to their daughter. What did they think was happening in this room? Maybe it was just a small thing, and I could get the job done in time for her to compete in her events. Maybe she'd seen some bubbleheaded starlet shoplift a bracelet or something.

"So… why don't you go ahead and tell me what you're planning to say on the stand?" I knew the drill with trial witnesses. Erase what they saw or heard—poof—the client walks free. I'd done it many times and helped exonerate who knew how many guilty people. I tried not to count—or wonder about what they'd done since I'd helped them walk free.

"Oh—right now?" she said. "You want me to tell you what he did to me? I didn't know I'd have to say it more than once. It's… embarrassing, you know?"

My throat tightened. She was the *victim* in the case? I hadn't bothered to ask Audun what kind of case this was—I never had in the past—I wasn't used to questioning him. It wasn't like it would've changed anything anyway if I did have forewarning about the kind of trial his client was facing. I was getting a sneaking suspicion I already knew, though—important client, underage girl. Yuck.

I swallowed back a gag and urged her on. "You won't have to repeat it. This is the only time you'll have to say it. I promise. Just start from the beginning, when you met him."

"Okay… well, I went to the concert with my friend Rachel. I was spending the night with her because her parents are cool about whatever time she wants to come in at night and we were planning to stay after the show and wait by the artists' exit to see if we could get an autograph. I was so excited because Aiden's my favorite singer. Or he *was*." She stopped and sniffled.

Aiden? Did she mean Aiden Ray? He wasn't Elven, but he was one of the top earning pop stars this year. If I wasn't mistaken, he'd won a Grammy as well. He was also about twenty-five years old. My belly did a sickening flop.

"Go on."

"We did wait after the show—we wanted to see him, like up close. There were lots of girls there, lined up, you know, outside the stage door near where his tour bus was parked. Some of them had pictures for him to sign or whatever. I didn't have anything like that—I was hoping he'd sign my hand. It started raining, but I didn't even care if I got wet. I just wanted to see him. I would have waited all night."

She sat on the edge of her chair, gripping the black leather seat cushion on either side of her spindly legs. Her eyes were far away, revisiting the scene in her mind.

"After about forty minutes the band came out. And then he did." Her voice choked with tears. "He was so beautiful in person… I started screaming and calling his name. He was signing everybody's things and taking selfies with them. And then he came to me. He tried to sign my hand with the marker, but I'd been out in the rain awhile. My skin was all wet, and the marker wouldn't work. I was so frustrated I started crying. And that's when he invited me to come into his bus."

"And you went?"

She nodded. "He said I could use a towel and dry off and then he could sign my hand in there. Of course I went."

"Did Rachel get on the bus, too?"

"No, the body guard said there was not enough room. He said only one person at a time could be in there with Aiden."

"I see. What happened when you got in the bus?"

"He went to the bathroom and got me a towel. He brought a robe, too, and said I could take off my wet clothes and put it on if I wanted to. He said it was his robe. I was… it was so nice of him to give me his robe. I thought about it. But I didn't want to take my clothes off. I was too scared. He shrugged like it was no big deal if I did or I didn't and then he took a soda out of the refrigerator for himself and one for me. He poured them into glasses and then he took a bottle of alcohol—I'm not sure what it was, if it was rum or something else. But he poured some of that in the glasses, too, and then he handed me one. 'To warm you up,' he said. I took a sip of it, but it tasted really bad—like strong, you know. So I put it down and used the towel to dry off my hand. He signed it for me, and I said thanks and told him I should go back outside because Rachel was waiting for me. He asked why I was leaving so soon."

She stopped talking here and seemed to consider something before continuing the story. "It was weird, but I *did* want to leave. I mean, I'd been dreaming of meeting him for like, years, and there I was alone with him, but all I wanted to do was leave. I was… afraid of him, of how he was looking at me. But he asked me to stay a little bit longer. He said how tired he was from the show, how lonely he was. That all he did was travel around and he never met anyone nice like me, that all he met were these skanky girls who were trying to have sex with him. He said I was different, I was nice to talk to. So… I relaxed a little bit. He asked me to sit beside him on the sofa there, and he talked to me. He told me about his parents getting divorced and how his mom was always pushing him to work when he was a kid and trying to turn him into a star. After a few minutes he held my hand. He asked me about my parents and my school and my friends. While I was talking, he leaned over and started kissing my neck. He told me I was beautiful—the most beautiful girl he'd seen out of all the places he'd been, and the nicest, and that made him… made him want me."

Crystal closed her eyes and let out a shuddering breath. "He put his hand on my face and turned it so I was looking into his eyes. He has the prettiest eyes, you know? And then he kissed me. He was a *really* good kisser—not like the boys at school. I liked him kissing me. I was freaking out a little inside like, *Aiden Ray is kissing me! Me!* I was so happy. And then he started doing more."

"What did he do?"

Her face reddened. "He was touching me and pushing me back till I was lying on the sofa. He moved so he was on top of me. He kept kissing me all the time. He pulled my shirt off and I let him, even though I wasn't sure I wanted to do that, but it was all happening really fast. And I liked him so much. I kept thinking I should stop, and I wanted to stop but I also didn't want to say anything, you know?"

I nodded, but actually I didn't know. Contrary to what we'd told Culley's father, this fourteen-year-old girl literally had more sexual experience than I did.

"Did anything happen that you *didn't* want, Crystal?"

Tears sprang to her eyes, and she nodded rapidly. "He opened up his pants. And then he reached under my skirt and tried to pull my underwear down." She sobbed. "I don't even know how it went that far. I wasn't planning to do all that with him. I freaked out. I started saying no over and over again."

She broke down and cried. Heart wringing in my chest, I reached out and patted her back.

"I'm so sorry… so sorry. Did he stop?"

She nodded and resumed her story, talking through tears. "He did. But he was so mad. He asked me if I was a virgin, and I told him yes. He asked me how old I was, and I told him fourteen, and he got even madder. Like, he stood up and started yelling, asking why the hell I hadn't told him I was fourteen. And I was crying and saying, 'I don't know. I don't know.' He never asked how old I was when we were talking. I didn't *know* he wanted to have sex when he invited me to come onto the bus. He told me to straighten up my clothes, and then he opened up the bus door and told his bodyguard to get rid of me. That's how he said it—'Get rid of her.'" She let out another sob. "And the thing is, I wasn't even going to tell anybody what happened. It's so *embarrassing*, and I don't like talking about it or even thinking about it. But when I didn't come out of the bus for a long time, Rachel left the arena and went home and told her parents where I was, and they told my parents. I had to tell them what happened—I couldn't help it, and they said it was assault and they were going to press charges. I just want it all to go away. I wish I hadn't gone on that bus with him. I wish I'd never met him. I never, ever want to have sex with *anyone* if that's what it's like."

"Does anyone else know? Anyone besides your parents and Rachel? Anyone from school?"

She shook her head. "Rachel doesn't even know—I told her all we did on the bus was talk. And that he gave me some alcohol."

"Okay." I knew what I had to do—to maintain my cover—*and* to help Crystal. I messaged Audun.

Let's get the parents in here next. I'll have to work on them, too.

Very well, he said, a satisfied expression crossing his face. He lifted the phone at his end of the table and said a few words to someone.

To Crystal, I said, "Listen to me now." I took her hand.

Her face glazed over in a trance-like dull expression as my glamour kicked in, and I continued. "You and Rachel went to that concert. You waited outside afterward to see Aiden, and he invited you to step into his bus to dry off your hand so he could sign it. You talked for a few minutes, and then he offered you an alcoholic drink, which made you feel uncomfortable. So you left the bus and went back out to look for Rachel. She had already left. That's all that happened. You enjoyed the concert, you got your hand signed, and you fulfilled your dream of meeting Aiden, but you didn't like him as much in person as you'd expected to." I squeezed her hand tighter. "He never touched you. You are still innocent, Crystal. One day when you meet the right guy and fall in love, you'll have a normal relationship. You won't hate sex or have any bad memories that haunt you about meeting Aiden Ray."

She nodded. When I took my hand from hers, she blinked several times and looked around. "Are we all done?"

"Yes. You did great."

Her bright smile faded slightly.

"Will Aiden be in trouble for giving me that alcohol?"

"Yes, I'm afraid so." I stood and gestured for Crystal to walk with me toward the conference room door. "That was not a smart thing for someone his age to do, and he's going to have to give you and your parents a large sum of money as a punishment to help him remember never to do it again."

That wasn't *all* I had planned for Mr. Aiden—not by a long shot. He was going to pay for what he'd done to Crystal and probably countless other girls. But I wouldn't state the rest of my intentions toward him aloud in Audun's presence. I couldn't let him know this was personal for me—or that I'd erased Crystal's haunting memories of the incident for *her* sake more than his client's.

As soon as she left the room, Audun was in my face. "Why did you tell her my client would be paying a settlement?" he demanded.

I kept my tone calm and even and matter of fact. "I had to leave her a partial memory because there were too many witnesses to her getting on that bus. If I removed everything, we'd have to bring in the bodyguard who saw her disheveled and upset, all the girls who saw her get on the bus, Rachel, her parents, and of course, Crystal's parents as well as anyone they might have told about their plans to come here today. They all know *something* happened. Now they'll never know what."

Through the glass walls I watched a secretary escort her parents toward us. I turned back to face Audun. "That's just to name a few of the potential witnesses who could show up if this goes to trial—too many potential loose ends. If your client is smart, he'll cough up some money for the Maggio family as fast as possible. He should be *thrilled* to settle out of court on a complaint of corrupting a minor by giving her alcohol. That won't even make the back page of the paper."

Audun visibly calmed. The conference room door opened, and the Maggio's came in, their eyes brimming with obvious confusion over why they were there.

"Thank you for meeting with us," I said, inviting them to take a seat at the table. "Your daughter is a brave girl to tell you the truth about what happened with such a big celebrity. I hope you're proud of her, and I think you'll be happy when you hear the settlement we're prepared to offer on your complaint concerning the alcohol he gave her."

"Alcohol?" Mr. Maggio slammed his hand on the tabletop. "This is about sexual assault. That man molested my little girl."

I placed my hand atop his, cringing inside at what I was about to do. This father was entitled to his fury. He was also suffering, as was his wife. I had to concentrate on the fact I would be removing that pain from them by erasing their memories of what Crystal had told them about the night with Aiden.

"No sir." I took Mrs. Maggio's hand as well. "Aiden Ray invited Crystal onto his bus, which was improper, and he gave her an alcoholic beverage, which was also wrong. You are right to be angry. But that is *all* that happened. That is the exact story she told you. And Mr. Ray is going to pay handsomely for that foolish error in judgment. He's agreed to settle with you out of court for five million dollars. You will never speak to the media or anyone about this. And in return, I can *promise you*, he will not be corrupting any other young girls."

When they came out of the memory-zapping spell, both Mr. and Mrs. Maggio were smiling. "Well, five million is most generous. I hope Aiden Ray has learned a lesson. I know Crystal has," Mrs. Maggio said.

"I think so, too," I said. "She's going to be fine."

They left the room, and Audun and I were alone again. Very slowly he strolled over and stood directly in front of me, looking into my eyes. "You *have* changed—and it's not just your relationship status with my son. You've started thinking on your own. I'm not sure I like it."

I lifted my chin, forcing myself to meet his gaze evenly, though inside all my nerves were scrambling backward to get away from him. "I'm growing up."

His eyes narrowed. "Yes. Well, next time you will consult me first instead of coming up with your own creative—and very costly—solution to a problem. Do not forget who's in charge here."

"Of course. I can't forget *anything*. May I go?"

He smirked. "See Miranda at the reception desk for a cash stipend and a new phone on your way out. I want to be able to reach you when I need you again."

I held my head high and maintained control until I'd rounded the corner, out of his line of vision. Then I ran to the ladies room and burst into muffled tears inside one of the stalls. Next time? No. I couldn't allow there to be a next time. I couldn't keep doing this to people—no matter their age. Now that I knew better, I had to get out of the Dark Court. I had to get away from Audun. And I had to find a way to stop him from using and hurting people.

He'd never stop—literally never. He'd continue in his evil ways his whole immortal life unless someone did something to stop him, and it looked like that someone would have to be me. I didn't know how I'd manage it yet, but I had to find a way to get the information the Light Court needed and then get away from here as soon as possible.

Chapter Thirteen
Roomies

Knocking at the door of my Manhattan flat felt like standing at the threshold of a past life.

The last time I'd been here about four months ago, I'd done some modeling jobs, gone out dancing with my roommates, and of course done Audun's bidding, following his instructions without thinking of any of it too much.

Now I couldn't stop myself from thinking. Had I done the right thing today with Crystal and her family? Could I have done anything any different? I supposed I could have refused to alter their memories. Audun would have punished me, but he'd likely have had them killed before allowing the girl to testify against his profitable client. At least this way they were alive, and they were happy. I hoped ignorance would be blissful for them.

I knocked again, harder this time, worried the volume of the TV blaring inside was drowning out the sound. I hadn't been able to reach any of my roommates by phone. After a minute, the door swung open, and Brenna's happy-surprise face filled the space.

"Ava! You're back in town. When did you get in?"

"Today."

I stepped inside and glanced around. The place hadn't changed at all since I'd left it, with its geometric printed carpet, spare, modern furniture, and narrow galley kitchen off to one side of the entryway. As always, it smelled like Chinese food in here, the one staple we could get any time of day or night, and cheaply.

"Anyone else in town?"

"Lena and Estelle—I don't think you've met her yet. She's in from Paris for a job. They're already out for the night. My rehearsal ran late, so I just got home and changed."

Brenna wore the kind of outfit that got you right in the door at the clubs, a sparkly gold strapless mini dress with swingy fringe at the bottom, perfect makeup, and huge hoop earrings. Her lean dancer's legs were enhanced by sky high strappy sandals, putting her well over six feet tall.

"I was going to join them—now you can come too." She smiled and picked up her purse from the table near the door.

I shook my head. "I can't go out tonight. I have to pack."

"What? Pack? Why?"

"I'm… moving in with Culley."

"Culley Rune? Wow—that is so awesome. He is *too* beautiful. I heard you two were together but I haven't seen you—I guess it's true. So, you're betrothed then?"

I raised my brows and blew out a breath. "Apparently so."

She laughed. "Don't even try to pretend you're not totally stoked. Any one of us would give up our glamours to bond with him. So when are you moving out?"

"He's expecting me tonight."

"Oh my God! Wow. You are so lucky. Okay, well let me text Lena and tell them I'm not coming. I'll stay and help you pack."

She pulled out her phone and tapped the screen. After a few seconds her face contracted in a regretful scrunch. "Ugh. There's a Broadway producer there at the bar I've been dying to work with. They said they're buying him drinks and holding him for me." She squinted an apologetic glance at me. "I'd die to get a part in his production of Franklin. And I want to do it on my own, you know? Not because somebody swayed him into hiring me. Will you be so mad if I go meet him?"

"No, of course not," I said. "You should go. Absolutely."

She grinned, her dark bobbed curls bouncing as she bounded across the kitchen to hug me. "You are the best. I'll see you around in the next day or two, right? Want to meet for lunch or something? That's if you can stand to drag yourself out of *bed*." Her eyebrows waggled and her voice put extra emphasis on *bed*.

I laughed at her silliness. "That sounds good. Have fun tonight. Good luck."

As she closed the door behind her, I crossed the small living/dining space to the sofa, searching between the cushions for the TV remote. The volume of the national news program was so loud I could hardly hear myself think. Brenna must've had it turned up so she could hear it in her bedroom while she got dressed. For reasons I could never fathom, she'd always been a news junkie, fascinated by the drama of everyday human life and problems.

The anchor's deep voice reverberated in my chest as I dropped to my knees to look under the sofa. "Police are baffled by the speed and severity of the new drug epidemic, and law enforcement lab technicians are working around the clock to determine the makeup of this powerful new designer drug…"

Failing to find the remote there, I went to the bedroom to look for it. Ah—there it was, on Brenna's unmade bed. Grabbing it, I raced back into the living area and clicked off the deafening report on humankind's latest miserable predicament. If I didn't succeed at discovering what Audun's latest plan was, they'd have a whole lot more to worry about than drugs and muggings—the return of fan pods, for instance, and eventually the return of Elven rule over their race.

I wondered how Lad and Ryann were doing in their quest to restore the tea production. And then I remembered my new phone. Pulling it from my purse, I dialed the number she'd given me.

"Hello?" Ryann's voice from Mississippi sounded so clear she could've been next door.

"Hi. It's Ava. I'm in New York. How are things there?"

She let out a heavy breath. "Still a mess. We couldn't salvage much from the factory, but we've set up a temporary tea production operation in Altum. Should be able to get out a shipment in a couple of days. It'll be small, but better than nothing. What are you doing in New York? I thought you and Culley were headed for California."

"I thought so, too, but plans changed. Be careful. I saw Audun today, and he mentioned something about having spies in Altum. I'd keep a close eye on anyone you let near the tea production there."

"Oh wow. Okay, thanks. I'll make sure I give everyone a good thorough reading with my glamour and warn Lad, too. So, how did it go with Audun?"

"I'm still alive." I gave a weak laugh. "So, I guess he doesn't know about my treason. Not yet, anyway."

"Culley didn't tell him anything?"

"No. Actually… actually he stepped in to protect me. I don't know. It was weird. I'm not sure what to think."

"I think he cares about you. In fact, I know he does."

"Um… I guess so. Well, anyway, I don't really have anything to report to you yet. Audun didn't say anything to indicate the Dark Council's next move. He did confirm they plan to overthrow Nox, though. Hopefully Audun will summon me again in the next few days, and he'll let something specific slip."

"Do you think he still trusts you?"

"I think so. He had me do a job for him, and he's confident of my loyalty because… well, he thinks Culley and I are bonded, so…"

There was a long pause. "Are you?"

"No," I yelped. Then more quietly, I said, "No. Culley told his father that… but…" And that's when it really hit me. My breaths shortened and picked up pace. "He lied. He lied to Audun. And Audun didn't seem to know."

"That's *interesting*," she said. "Listen, I have to get off the phone. Call Lad and tell him what you told me. Let me give you his number."

I scribbled it down before we said good-bye then took a seat at one of the kitchen counter stools and focused on breathing normally. *Culley lied to Audun.* For me. But even more shocking than the fact he'd trick his father to protect me—the lie had *worked*.

Was Audun's power slipping? Or was there a loophole? Maybe his son was immune. Or maybe he'd inherited his father's gift.

What if Culley was not only able to make people see what they wanted to see, he could make them hear what they wanted to hear? Oh my. That would be an incredibly dangerous combination. Right now Culley was rather indifferent to all the political intrigue of the Dark Court. He was the king of *live and let live.* But if he ever got fully on board with Audun's plans, he would be a formidable enemy.

Over the next three hours I packed up the clothes and personal items I kept in the flat. It shouldn't have taken me that long. For one thing, I had to call Mother and explain why she wouldn't be getting guaranteed lifetime support from Audun, thanks to my failure in Altum. Sadly, I couldn't tell her the truth, and she wouldn't have cared anyway. All she could think of was what she "deserved."

For another—I dragged my feet a bit. The truth was, I wasn't exactly eager to show up on Culley's doorstep with my life in a box. He'd no doubt expect me to be grateful to him for saving my butt, and I was. But I wasn't *that* grateful.

Not enough to actually bond with him, if that's what he was expecting. I wasn't going to do that with *anyone*. I was still planning to leave the Dark Court as soon as I could. Bonding with Culley would mess up all my plans for independence. It wouldn't be fair to him anyway. He needed a bond-mate who was actually planning to stick around. He'd only get one chance, after all. He shouldn't waste it on me.

My new phone rang, startling me with its foreign ring tone. I didn't recognize the number but I answered it anyway.

"Hello?"

"Are you ready to move into your new home?"

"Oh, Culley. Yes. I just finished packing."

"Excellent. There's a car waiting for you downstairs. I know you have no money for a cab. I'll instruct the driver to come up and help you bring your things down."

"You're not in the car?"

"No—I have some… things to do. I'll be in late tonight. The driver knows the address. It's apartment four on the eleventh floor. Make yourself at home. Choose any bathroom, any room you'd like to put your things."

"Okay." There was an awkward silence. "Thanks."

He hesitated a moment before replying. "Sure. See you later, Angel."

A knock at the door signaled the arrival of the driver/moving man and the beginning of my new life in New York, as short-lived as it might be.

Chapter Fourteen
Ruined

Culley's apartment was beautiful. And spacious. So spacious, in fact, I hardly saw him for the next week.

Instead of chasing me around and demanding his "bond-mate rights" as I'd feared, he stayed gone most of the time, coming and going at all hours of the day and night with hardly a word to me. Like me, he had a few modeling jobs. But even at night when he wasn't working, he was "out" and less than forthcoming about *where* "out" was. Every night since I'd moved in I went to bed alone in the apartment, unable to wait up for whenever it was he managed to make it home.

It was for the best, really. So much better than having him there all the time making provocative remarks, or worse, making me feel sorry for him. It was lonely though.

I did have lunch with Brenna once, and later in the week invited her and Lena and Estelle over for drinks at my new "home."

"Wow, this place is incredible," Lena said, wandering from window to window, taking in the view of Central Park. It was nearly Thanksgiving, and the trees below were gorgeous, a colorful scarf spread out right in the middle of the gray city.

"Where eese heese bedroom?" Estelle asked, her lilting Parisian accent making even that nosy question sound elegant. She had been in New York only a couple of weeks, and her English wasn't perfect. Of course it was a hell of a lot better than my French.

"Estelle—it's *their* bedroom," Brenna chided. "He's off the market. You know that." She looked over at me with an apologetic glance, as if her roommate's predatory behavior was somehow her fault.

"Sorry," Estelle said, not sounding the least bit sorry. "Ee doesn't act bonded. I see eem out at zee dance clubs every night, smiling at all the girls, boys too, dancing, drinking…" She slid a glance over at me. "… having conversations in dark corners."

Though it was none of my business what Culley did every night—in plain view or in dark corners—my face heated until I felt like I'd drunk way more of my mojito than I actually had. I stepped into the kitchen and picked up the tray of appetizers I'd prepared for us all.

"Come have a seat in here," I called, carrying the tray to a wide low table in front of the sectional sofa. This room as well had a gorgeous view.

Unfortunately, it also had a giant TV, which Brenna zeroed in on with glee. "Oh, you are so lucky. Look at this baby." She picked up the remote and turned it on, skipping through channels until it landed on a local New York news program. Of course.

"Also breaking tonight, city hospitals are reporting another round of overdoses in what's now being called the "S Scourge."

The stylish newscaster had a graphic over one shoulder that looked like a pill emblazoned with the letter S. "Authorities say it's the fastest-moving and most addictive drug epidemic they've ever encountered," she said. "New York officials are moving quickly to assemble an S task force to locate the source of the drug and working together with officials up and down the East Coast to target and shut down distribution. Donald Trump has already called a press conference on the matter, blaming foreign immigrants for the influx of the powerful and incredibly popular club drug."

"Where can *I* get some?" Estelle asked with a wicked grin.

"Estelle!" Lena chided. "You know Audun's strictly forbidden us to use it."

Estelle giggled. "You Americans are so provincial. And Audun is about as fun as your police. What about free will? If I want to do something, I should be able to. Why should the humans get all the fun? And if they want to use it, let them use it. Let them *all* O.D.—who cares?"

I said nothing but stared at the TV screen as if thoroughly interested. But in my mind, the girls' conversation replayed. Audun had forbidden his subjects to use S.

So he was aware of it. Why had he not included me in this sanction? Maybe he knew I spent my time either working or home alone. Maybe he assumed I knew better than to take drugs. Maybe I was out of sight out of mind as far as he was concerned. That would have suited me very well, thank you—except that I needed to get information from him. Which meant I needed to see him. Maybe I should request a meeting, make up some concern about my mother as an excuse.

The phone rang loudly through the apartment. I hated the ringer on that thing. Not only did I have to hear it frequently—and the answering machine that went with it—but it was loud enough to be clearly audible even over the TV and our conversation in the other room.

"Aren't you going to get that?" Lena asked after several rings.

I shook my head. "No. It's not for me. It rings all day and night. It's always for Culley. The machine will get it."

The girls all went quiet as Culley's recorded voice echoed down the hall. "Hey. It's me. But I guess you knew that. Leave a message, and I'll try to ring you back later."

"God I love that accent," said Brenna.

"Shhh," said Estelle and Lena together, both leaning toward the hallway, listening.

The beep sounded, followed by a very typical message. "Hi Culley. This is Lilly. From Marquee Nightclub? I haven't heard from you in a while, and I just wanted to say hi. I'm available tonight if you want to stop by my place or something. Or I could meet you out somewhere. Okay then, hope to hear from you soon. Bye."

The other girls looked at me.

"*That* happens all day and night?" Brenna said. "You should start answering that phone and tell those skanks to stay away from your man."

"Absolument!" Estelle agreed. "I would not stand for theese."

Flushing furiously, I stood and gathered the used plates and silverware. "It's his business. It's no big deal."

What I couldn't tell them was it really wasn't my concern. I would be leaving Culley soon. It was good that he had so many other girls interested in him. Really, it was.

But late that night after the girls had left and he still wasn't home, I had to admit to myself it did bother me. It was annoying. Especially when the phone rang at nearly midnight. This time I did march toward it, intending to pick it up and tell whichever little club girl was calling to at least have some manners about the late hour. Before I could reach it, the call went to the answering machine. It was not a sexy feminine plea but a man's voice.

"It's Anders. I didn't uh… see you tonight. I don't know if you came by already or what." The sounds of music and voices hummed in the background. The man was nearly shouting over the din, and he sounded decidedly un-sober. "I'm at Cielo. Some friends of mine are here, too, and we're ready to ride the S train, so look for me if you stop by."

My heart seized. The S train. Was he talking about S— the drug on the news? Was Culley doing *drugs*? Maybe that's why he stayed out late every night, why he'd changed so suddenly and grown distant. Maybe he'd gotten caught up in the epidemic that was sweeping New York and apparently the entire East Coast.

I'd rarely heard of Elves doing drugs—it didn't affect them strongly enough to be… enjoyable, or whatever drugs were supposed to be. But the news report did say this drug seemed to be different, powerful and highly addictive. Maybe some scientist had developed a super-drug that could affect even the Elven body and mind? It made me sick to think of Culley falling under the influence of something so insidious. I would talk to him about it the next time I managed to get him alone.

The sound of the front door opening caused me to jump out of my skin.

"Culley?" I called, scurrying toward the entry hall.

It was him. His back was to me as he fastened the deadbolt. His shoulders were slumped. He looked exhausted.

"Culley… where have you been? Are you okay?"

He spun around as if just hearing me. A wide grin spread across his face and he moved toward me, staggering slightly. *Oh no. He is on drugs.*

But when he reached me, it was the odor of alcohol that met my nose. He slid his arms around my waist and lifted me off my feet. "There's the little wifey—still awake. Were you waiting up for me?" he slurred. Putting me down, he staggered past me toward the kitchen. "Ha—I'll bet you missed me *so much*. Probably had a party." He must have spotted the dishes and cocktail glasses on the counter because he added, "You *did* have a party, cheeky monkey. And I wasn't invited. Big surprise."

For some reason his inebriated state irritated me. "Yes. I did have some friends over because I wanted to have *someone* around to talk to. You're never here. Is this how you always live—or are you avoiding me?"

He spun around to face me again, knocking himself off balance then gripping the counter edge to steady himself. "Now why would I do that? What kind of drongo would avoid *you?*" He gave my pajama-clad figure a lecherous once over. "I mean, with a *loving* fiancée waiting at home, a man would have to be a fool to stay out all night."

What was going on with him? He was acting so weird. And he didn't seem to be under the influence of drugs. I'd seen my fair share of drunk people, and Culley was a classic case tonight.

I stepped forward, putting myself directly in front of him, squarely in his line of vision, so he couldn't avoid the question. "Why *do* you stay out so late? What are you doing every night?"

He grinned again. "Are you worried about me, love? Come here." He dragged me closer with a big warm hand. "I'll show you what I'm *not* doing out there."

And then his hand was at the base of my spine, pulling me in to his body. He let go of the counter, and his back fell against the refrigerator door, leaning against it for support. Through no choice of my own, I went with him.

Before I could protest, Culley's mouth descended to mine, and he administered an alcohol-flavored but very skillful kiss.

My hands went to his chest to push myself off of him, but he clamped a hand on the back of my head and deepened the kiss. My heart rate tripled. *Wow.* This was... this was unexpected. And he was a great kisser. It was confusing. I'd felt abandoned, hurt by his complete lack of attention, and now here he was giving me every ounce of his attention and shocking me with the pleasure of it all.

Ripping his lips from my mouth, Culley moved to my neck, traversing the length of it with hot, wet kisses that stole my breath and all the strength from my legs. He spoke in between the strokes of his tongue on my skin. "I'm not out there doing it because all I can think about is being here doing this with you. You've ruined me... ruined me. And you don't even *want* me."

A desperate laugh escaped his throat as his fingers wrapped around my shoulders and set me away from him. "Every other girl in this stinking, overcrowded city wants me—and you think I'm shit. Well, you're right."

138

Pushing me to the side, he staggered out of the kitchen and down the hall toward his bedroom.

I watched him go, thinking about his statement. He was wrong. I didn't think he was shit. I was surprised by how much I'd grown to like him. And after that kiss—well, he was surprising me in all sorts of ways.

But I couldn't talk to him when he was in this state. And I *couldn't* stay with him.

Could I?

Would he consider coming *with* me? Helping me? He said he thought about kissing me all the time. He said I'd "ruined" him. Maybe it was enough. I didn't love him, which would have been a nice prerequisite to marriage and bonding, but I did like him, and we were in similar situations—both lonely—both miserable under his father's thumb. Maybe the two of us could set out on our own… together.

I'd wait for him to sober up then present the idea in the morning. The worst he could do was laugh in my face. No—check that—the worst he could do would be to tell Audun I planned to desert the Dark Court. But I didn't think Culley would do that. He'd already proved his unwillingness to expose me to his father's legendary wrath.

I'd be asking him to go one step further—and choose me over his name and position.

* * *

That conversation did not happen the next morning or even the next day. I had a modeling job and left the apartment before Culley woke up. At least I assumed he was sleeping. His door was still closed. No doubt it had been a rough night—he was probably hung *all* the way over and feeling horrible. I'd tried to avoid clanking dishes in the kitchen and tiptoed out, shutting the apartment door gently behind me.

When I got home from work, the apartment was empty. There was a note on the counter, scribbled in Culley's handwriting.

> *Sorry about last night. Bombed out drunk. Didn't mean it. I'll be out late—don't wait up.*

The air whooshed from my lungs, and I sat hard onto the bar stool. Well, it was a good thing I hadn't proposed my let's-run-off-together plan. I read the words again.

Didn't mean it.

He could have fooled me. It certainly sounded and *felt* like he meant it last night. This topic wasn't closed yet. There was more going on between us than a mutual living space and fake life-bond. And the next time I saw him, I planned to make him admit it.

CHAPTER FIFTEEN
REPORTING FOR DUTY

Over the next few days, Culley was a ghost, coming in after I'd fallen asleep and disappearing from the apartment before I woke. I only knew he'd been there because food had vanished from the refrigerator. The night before Thanksgiving he didn't come home at all.

I got up before dawn Thanksgiving morning, grinning, because I knew his effort to avoid me was at an end. Today he'd have no choice. We'd been booked to shoot a commercial together for a jewelry company—an engagement ring ad, actually. The backdrop would be the Macy's Thanksgiving Day Parade.

The two of us would spend the day acting like a couple in love enjoying the parade. I was sure the casting agent thought he'd made a brilliant choice of models because our real-life engagement had made it on to some of the entertainment shows and online sites. Little did he know we weren't even speaking to each other.

I'd just gotten out of the shower when my phone rang. It was Audun's secretary, asking me to come to his office for an early meeting.

"I have a shoot today," I explained.

"He's aware of that. It'll be quick. He says it's important."

There was no way to say no. Not if I valued keeping my secret—and my life.

I assured her I'd be right over. "Of course. If it's important to him, it's important to me." *Good little soldier, reporting for duty.*

This time after I checked in with the receptionist I walked back to his office alone, stepping inside when the doors opened. Hopefully we'd stay *indoors* today to discuss our business. Hopefully he wouldn't dangle me over the edge of the building when I had an on-camera job in an hour. And *hopefully* he'd give me something I could use so I could get the hell out of this city and away from him.

"Ah, Ava. Come in dear." Audun rose from his perch behind his desk and approached me. Gesturing toward the sofa in front of the lit fireplace, he said, "Let's sit over here and chat. It won't take long. I have a new job for you."

Great. I followed his instructions and sat at one end of the sofa, working to keep my expression neutral, my posture confident.

"How are things with Culley?"

I couldn't lie. Things weren't that great. But I was hoping they *would* be. "I haven't seen enough of him lately, but it'll be good to do a shoot with him today. I'm looking forward to it." Whew. That was true. Just not for the reason Audun thought it was.

"Very good," he said. "When you have finished with that, I'll need you to stop by the New York Police Department."

"The police?"

"Yes. There's a detective named Ballard working in the 19th precinct. You'll ask to meet with him, tell him you have some pertinent information on the S 'scourge.'" He rolled his eyes at the dramatic label. "When you get into his office, you'll remove any memories he has of his investigation. And erase his files."

I sat for a moment, stunned. "Okay… so… you *don't* want the police to bust the S dealers."

He laughed. "Of course not. Why would you think that?"

"Well, my roommates—my former roommates—told me you'd warned them against using it. I thought you weren't a fan."

He grinned widely. Though his face was extremely attractive, the effect of that smile wasn't beautiful. It was frightening.

"Oh I'm more than a fan. S is my baby. It's a miracle. It's the answer we've been looking for. Who cares about controlling human minds with fan pods when we can wipe out huge numbers of their race with overdoses and drug addiction? It's the most addictive substance in existence—it's already on its way to replacing cocaine and heroin and oxycodone in the cities where it's available. And we're making it available in as many places as possible as quickly as possible. Soon there'll be so few humans left alive or sober enough to fight us, they'll have no hope of resisting when we re-establish our reign. The world will return to us once more with just enough humans remaining to serve our needs."

He said it matter-of-factly, as if it were all so obvious. And so desirable. Maybe it was—to him and his devoted followers. To me it was revolting. There was no way I could be a part of this. He had to be stopped. I needed information to do that. Apparently now that I was "eternally bonded" to his son, he trusted me enough to hand it over.

"So you plan to take S distribution worldwide then."

"Of course. It won't even be that hard. They can't get enough of it—of course making it cheaper than chips doesn't hurt. The money is of no consequence." He waved his hand through the air as if shooing away gnats. In this case, the gnats were human lives.

As long as he was spilling information so freely, I might as well get some details. "I never even heard of S before a couple weeks ago. Where does it come from? What's it made of?" I asked.

Audun's eyes narrowed in an assessing gaze. Apparently he didn't trust me *completely*. "You are certainly taking an interest in the family business. And while I'd love to discuss it with you further, I know you need to go. There's a cab waiting for you downstairs to take you to the shoot location. Pay detective Ballard a visit this evening and report back to me tomorrow."

Understanding I'd been dismissed, I stood and walked to the door.

"Oh and Ava," Audun called.

I twisted to look back at him.

"Enjoy the parade."

Chapter Sixteen
An Open Door

The cab ride to the shoot location took about three times longer than it should have because of the insane parade day traffic.

"All these tourists," the cab driver yelled, throwing a hand up in frustration toward the pedestrian-packed street in front of us. "Which streets *aren't* blocked off?"

Taking advantage of the delay, I placed a call to Lad. He and Nox needed to know what Audun's plans were regarding S distribution and how he intended to use the highly addictive drug to decimate and control the human population.

I knew as soon as Lad answered the phone he wasn't in Altum. For one thing, he couldn't get a signal underground. For another, the smooth voice of Frank Sinatra sang in the background, and I heard women's voices laughing.

"Hi Lad. It's Ava. Where are you?"

"I've been invited to celebrate American Thanksgiving with Ryann's family. We're all in the kitchen. I'm... chopping things."

I giggled to myself, picturing the King of the Light Court slicing and dicing celery at the kitchen counter. Like my clan, the Light Elves didn't celebrate the holiday. But the homey mental picture almost made me wish we all did. I'd seen it portrayed on TV and in movies, and it always seemed rather idyllic to me—a large family gathered around a bountiful table, expressing gratitude for the good things in their lives.

"Can you step outside for a minute or something? I have some information for you."

"Yes. Sure. Hold on." All I heard was his breathing for a minute then a door closing. The chirp of a bird on his end of the line pinged my heart with a sudden sweet sadness and a sense of homesickness for the place, which was crazy. I'd spent all of a week there.

"Okay, what's going on?" he asked.

"I know what Audun's plan is—he's distributing a new drug—it's highly addictive and use of it is spreading really fast. It's called S. I've seen reports on the news about mass overdoses. His goal is to spread it far and wide and let the humans basically kill themselves off with it or become weak and helpless because they're addicted. That way no one will fight back when he launches his plan to overtake them."

"That is bad news. But it's good to know. Thank you Ava. I hope you didn't endanger yourself to get this

AMY PATRICK

information. Do you know where it's coming from? Where it's made?"

"Not yet. But later today I'm going to speak to a police detective who's been looking into it. I'm supposed to erase his memories about it, but I'll gather all the information I can from him first. I'll let you know as soon as I find out something useful."

"Good job. Thank you. I'll inform Nox and Vancia and Ryann." There was a creaking noise and a muffled voice then Lad came back on. "Hold on, Ryann's here. She'd like to speak with you a minute."

There was a pause before she came on the line. "Ava? Hi. Are you okay?"

"Yes. I'm fine. I'm making some progress. I'm sure Lad will tell you everything."

"Well, I hope you're safe. And I wanted to tell you… the minute you finish there, we want you to come here—to Altum. There'll be too much danger after this for you inside the Dark Court, and we've already prepared a place for you—"

"No," I blurted. "I mean, thank you, but I couldn't."

There was no way I could leave New York without telling Culley what his evil father was up to. Once he knew the truth, he'd feel the same way I did. He'd want to get away and never look back. He might even want to leave *with me*.

And the one place we couldn't go together was Altum. Not after what he'd done to Lad and Ryann. The ancient underground kingdom wasn't where I belonged anyway. I was too used to modern conveniences and interacting with the human world. I dreamed of a nice sunny spot somewhere I could grow that little vegetable garden of mine.

"I'm going to do some traveling before settling anywhere," I told her. "I'm not sure where I'll land after that." In all honesty, there was nowhere I wanted to travel more than back to Deep River, Mississippi. Its dark, rich earth and slow, easy pace of life called to me somehow.

And then of course there was…

"Asher was asking about you," Ryann said.

My heart started pounding. "You saw him?"

"Yes. He's worried about you. He wanted to know where to find you. The boy's got it bad."

Oh this *was* bad. So why did it make my heart so happy to hear her words?

"What did you tell him?"

"Not much. I mentioned you were in New York City, working, but no details or anything. The last thing we want is for someone innocent like him to get involved in all this, right?"

"Right. Absolutely," I said quickly.

There was a pause on the other end of the line. "You sure about that? You sound kind of—"

"Listen, Ryann, I've got to go. I'm late for a job, and my cab just got here. I've got to pay the guy and get out."

"Okay then, but if you ever change your mind…"

"Bye," I wheezed and opened the cab door.

A cacophony of noise filled my ears. Car horns, voices, tubas, and drums all mixed together in bright, happy anticipation of the parade beginning. Wrapped up in my conversations with Lad and Ryann, I hadn't really paid attention to the sights outside the moving cab, but now I looked up and gasped.

Television coverage hadn't done the balloons and floats justice—the vivid colors, the massive size, the attention to detail—it took my breath away and made me feel like I was walking through a dreamscape as I made my way through the crowd toward a small restaurant the production company had rented out to use for hair and wardrobe and a general shoot headquarters.

Sometimes on location shoots we'd have a trailer for that kind of thing, but this one was unique. And there was no way anyone would be squeezing a trailer onto the parade route today. I reached the glass door of the deli and pushed it open, breathing a sigh of relief as I stepped inside.

I was actually only about five minutes late, though you wouldn't have known it from the over-the-top reaction of the director.

"Oh my gawd," she squawked. Her crazy gray hair bobbed up and down as she stalked toward me. "The princess has arrived everyone. Let's all take a minute to curtsy and then get some freakin' wardrobe and makeup on her. The parade doesn't last all day people. Nice of you to join us, Miss Morten. If it wasn't for your gorgeous fiancé over there talking us down from the ledge, I'd have fired your narrow ass already and picked some girl out of the crowd for him to 'propose' to—he's the only thing anyone will be looking at anyway."

"And the ring," a man piped up from the back of the room. He wore a suit and tie that screamed "ad agency" and held a small velvet box.

"Right," the director growled. "The ring—of course."

Tables and chairs had been pushed from the center of the room toward the walls to make room for clothing racks and equipment. No doubt the portable set lights were already set up wherever it was we'd be filming out on the route. I scanned the room, looking for Culley.

When my eyes landed on him, he raised one hand in a lackluster acknowledgement without taking his gaze from his phone, scrolling over the screen as the hair stylist worked on his already-perfect platinum locks.

Okay, so he won't even look at me. Fine. Two could play at that game. I could tell he was affected by my presence whether he wanted me to know or not. His free hand was clenched on the chair arm, making the muscles in his forearm and hand stand out in sharp relief. His jaw was tight, too, in that way I'd observed during our long road trip whenever I hit a nerve with my questions. And the fact he *wouldn't* look at me and had avoided me altogether since our inebriated kiss—that had to mean *something.*

I would find out, and I'd do it today, because tomorrow would be too late. If all went according to my new plan, I wouldn't be in this city come nightfall.

Chapter Seventeen
You May Kiss the Bride

Once we were both completely styled, the action moved outside where the parade had gotten underway. It was crazy, but I guessed that's what they wanted. The concept of the ad campaign was to capture the excitement and magic of the event and encourage people—shoppers—to see the romantic side of the holiday season.

It was hard to achieve a romantic vibe with Culley refusing to even look my direction whenever the cameras weren't rolling. But I did my best to get through the shoot, vowing nothing would keep me from speaking with him alone once it was over.

When the cameras *were* rolling, we did our best to fake happy coupledom, but Culley's eyes never met mine. He appeared to be looking at my ear during any shot that was supposed to be a romantic gaze.

"Come on, people, we're in *love* here," complained the director. "Show me *something* before the jolly fat man makes his appearance. Why am I paying a freaking fortune for this?" she asked her assistants who shook their heads in that *Don't ask me* way.

Culley shot a brief, murderous glare in her direction, then finally looked directly at me.

Let's get this over with, okay?

I nodded. What was his problem? A few days ago he'd been perfectly content to be in a cramped car with me, to share a hotel room. Now he apparently considered it too much of a hassle to even be near me.

Following the director's instructions, Culley and I laughed and held hands as we watched the parade. I leaned my head on his shoulder in a contented way.

"Now touch her cheek," the director said.

Culley lightly placed his fingers on my jaw and turned my face to meet his gaze. And this time his eyes locked onto mine. The look in them nearly stopped my heart. It was stunning, paralyzing. He looked like he wanted to carry me off somewhere far from the parade and keep me there a long, long time. My heart did start beating again, but now at a blistering pace. Either he'd suddenly developed some major acting chops, or this guy *wanted* me. He was impossible to figure out.

"Good. Cut. Re-set cameras," the director barked. "It's time for the money shot."

I stood off to the side, my legs wobbly and my breathing erratic as I waited for them to make everything ready for the proposal scene.

We stepped back into frame, and the director said, "Action."

As the colorful floats and costumed performers passed behind us, Culley dropped to one knee and pulled the velvet box from his pocket. I covered my mouth with one hand and acted surprised, and he opened the box to reveal the ring.

There was no dialogue in this ad. Instead, Culley raised his brows in a questioning way, and I nodded vigorously with tears in my eyes, smiling hugely. Then he stood and swept me up in a tight, joyous hug of celebration.

"Better," the director yelled. "Much better. But the script calls for a kiss. We're not trying to get *friends* to buy rings here—the target audience is lovers. No hugs."

Once more we played out the proposal and acceptance. Culley rose, lifted me to my toes, and this time he kissed me.

And kissed me.

And kissed me.

If he was acting, call the Oscar committee, because *wow*. I felt his kiss in every molecule of my body. By the time it ended, I was trembling all over, barely aware of the music and crowd and film crew.

When we pulled apart, I stared at him, unable to tear my gaze away from his fierce blue eyes. There was something new in them, a question, a longing. I wasn't sure what was happening. He hadn't let me go yet.

The director laughed out loud. "Cut. Cut. Before he eats her alive." She laughed again. "When you turn it on Mr. Rune, you *really* turn it on. That's a wrap."

Culley released me. Without a word, he spun on his heel and walked away, pushing through the thick crowd. What the hell?

"Santa's coming," a young boy squealed, and the kids around me started jumping, making it more difficult to follow my "fiancé," who was apparently intent on escaping.

"Culley wait," I called to his back. "Wait for me. I want to talk to you."

He stopped and turned back around, wearing a stern expression that was nearly a frown. "What?"

I reached him and looked up into his shuttered gaze. What was going on inside that crazy-beautiful head of his? He avoided me for days, kissed me silly, looked at me like he never wanted me out of his sight, and now he was running away?

"We need to talk. Can we go somewhere…" I glanced around at the mad scene. "…quieter?"

"We can talk at home… later." He twisted and tried to walk away again.

My hand caught his arm, stopping him. He turned back to me.

"No," I said. "Because I know what's going to happen— you won't *come* home. You're avoiding me. Why?"

For a moment he stared intensely into my eyes, and then he glanced away. "Did you have something to say to me, Ava? Because if not, I have to go."

Ava. He'd called me Ava. Not "Angel." Not "love."

"Culley." I blew out a frustrated breath. If he wouldn't talk to me, at least he was listening. I had to tell him what his father was up to, and this might be my only chance. I couldn't leave town with no explanation, and I couldn't let him go on thinking his father was anything but what he was—a monster.

"I had a conversation with Audun this morning."

His gaze whipped back to me. "About what?"

"He asked me to speak to a police detective who's investigating the S epidemic—you know, the drug? S?"

His lips tightened. "Yes, I've heard of it."

"Audun told me to erase the detective's files and his memories. He wants the drug to flourish and the addiction to spread. He's behind it, Culley. He admitted it to me."

"And?"

"*And...* I can't do it. I can't be a part of his evil plans anymore. Did you know earlier this week he forced me to make an assault case against a pop star go away? The victim was fourteen. *Fourteen.* I can't do it anymore. And it doesn't even matter if he tracks me down and has me killed—I couldn't live with myself if I kept doing this stuff anyway. I'm leaving. I'm leaving New York tonight." I paused. "I want you to come with me."

The longing in Culley's eyes was real—I knew it was. And yet the words that came out of his mouth denied it. "I can't leave. My place is here. So is yours. How were you planning to go, by the way? You have no car."

"I… I don't know. I'll take the bus or something." I hadn't really thought out the how part. The why part I had down. "You can't stay here, Culley. You don't want to be involved in a drug ring. You're not like your father."

His arms folded across his chest. "How do you know? Maybe I'm exactly like him."

"You're not. I believe you have a good heart. All *he* cares about is power, at any cost. He has to be stopped—at the very least you need to get away from him to protect yourself. And why would you stay? He's been a terrible father—you told me that. Come with me. If you stay here you could be in danger because you lied to him about us… *somehow*."

His face swam with pain. He swallowed hard, his Adam's apple moving down his throat in a rapid jerk. "You wouldn't even ask me to go… if you really knew me."

The quiet words stunned me. It took me a moment to recover. I took one of his big hands in both of mine. "Culley. Look at me."

Reluctantly, he brought his eyes to meet mine.

"You're wrong. I do know you—"

He shook his head. "You don't. No one does. You'd hate me if you knew the things I've done."

"Do you think *I'm* perfect? No—you know better. Everyone's done something they're ashamed of, but it's not too late. I like the part of you I do know. And it could be even more. I think I could fall in love with you, Culley, in time. But you *have* to let me in. You don't want to spend your life alone.

157

And I can't spend my life with an image, with a facade. You have to let me see the real you—all of you." I hesitated before going further. But it was now or never for us. "Show me what you really look like," I challenged.

His eyes widened then went hard as ice. "If I… let you see me, all of me… I'll lose you."

"Culley… you're going to lose me if you *don't*."

He lifted his other hand to join it with mine. We stood there for several moments, his eyes on our locked fingers. The indecision in the air was as palpable as one of the oversized balloons bobbing down the avenue.

Finally Culley spoke. "Where's the ring you used to wear?" His thumb rubbed over my bare finger. "The one with the Elven phrase for—"

"I lost it. It… fell off." At some point I'd tell him that I had—for some reason I could not explain myself—given my father's ring to Asher. This was not the time, though.

Culley's gaze lifted to mine, and he studied my face with an expression of sorrow and something else—disappointment?

"You know, Angel, you don't let me see the real you, either," he whispered.

"Ava!" A voice in the distance called my name. At first I assumed it was some parent searching for a child of the same name who'd wandered away in the post-parade exodus. But then I heard it again, stronger, and the voice was familiar.

"Ava."

I whirled around, and my eyes searched the crowd for—

"Asher," I gasped. "Oh my God. What is he doing here?"

Chapter Eighteen
The Real Me

"That's what I'd like to know." Culley stepped in front of me and strode forward to meet Asher's approaching figure. "A bit far from the farm, aren't you mate?"

Asher ignored Culley completely, side-stepping him to get to me.

"Ava," he said again, beaming. He grabbed me in a bear hug and swung me around. "Oh man are you a sight. I can't believe I found you in this crowd—I've never seen so many people in my whole life. I spotted the film crew, and one of the techs told me you'd gone this way."

When he set me down again, I fell back a step and stared at him, hardly able to believe my eyes. He was such a contrast to the residents of the city I'd been immersed in for the past week. Wearing his ever-present boots and jeans with a t-shirt, his only nod to the Northern climate was a brown leather jacket that hung open to reveal his wide chest and lean torso.

"How did you… what are you…"

"I went by your modeling agency when I got to town yesterday and asked if they might know how I could get in touch with you. The lady at the desk was real nice." He winked and flashed that mind-bending smile of his, and I knew exactly how he'd managed to get information out of the *nice* lady at the desk. No doubt it was the same "nice" lady who hardly said two words to me and the other female models whenever we were there. But could I blame her? Asher's smile would melt even the iciest of Manhattan receptionists. She'd probably tried to talk him into sitting for some shirtless portraits while he was there, too, so she could save them for her personal use.

"She said she couldn't tell me where you lived, but she did mention you'd be here shooting a commercial today," he explained. "And here you are."

I nodded, feeling dazed. "And here *you* are. Aren't you supposed to be in school or something?"

"Thanksgiving break. I thought it was about time to see the world north of Virginia." He paused for effect. "And I came to bring you home."

I blinked. Blinked again. "What?"

"Ryann mentioned you might be in need of some transportation back to Deep River. Big Red's parked in a garage a couple blocks over. Can you believe they charge fifty dollars for an hour of parking here?"

"Asher… I don't know what to say… I…"

"So, I guess you won't be needing that bus after all," Culley quipped. "Or me for that matter."

I turned away from Asher's beautiful smile to see Culley's equally beautiful scowl. He was not happy to see the human boy here. That was obvious. But then he did the strangest thing. He stepped forward and gave Asher a friendly back-slap. And a tight smile.

"I suggest you two get on the road before all these tourists do. I would imagine you don't have much experience navigating city traffic. Take 34th here to 495. It's your fastest route to 95 South. Although you'll probably want to stop by and pick up her things first. Ava can give you the address of the apartment. You can park in the fire lane out front for about ten minutes before the doorman will report you."

Appearing surprised, Asher studied Culley's face for a moment, then reading no malice or deception there, he extended his hand. "Thanks man. Appreciate you looking out for her while she was here. You ready to go, Ava?"

My gaze bounced back and forth between them. This was all happening so fast. It was amazing to see Asher. I'd missed him more than I'd even realized. But the thought of leaving Culley behind—it seemed wrong to abandon him here. Especially now that I knew his father's nefarious plans. No doubt he'd try to suck Culley into them. In spite of our differences, I felt a connection to him. And yet he appeared to be more than willing to hand me over to Asher.

My heart was bouncing around in my chest like an over-hit ping pong ball on a concrete floor.

I didn't say I was going with him, I said to Culley mind to mind as I took a step toward him. *I'm… not sure what I should do.*

He took a step backward. "You should go."

He was sending me away. I could hardly believe it. Tears began streaming down my face, shocking me, and from the looks of it, Culley, too. His mouth fell open, and his eyelids flared.

I don't think I can leave you, I told him. How could I? Culley had refused to open up to me—so far—but I had a feeling his diamond-hard façade was close to cracking. And that what was inside the tough shell would be worth the wait. What was inside was certainly too valuable to let his father destroy it.

Culley and I held fervent eye contact for a long moment. Then the heat in his gaze frosted over, like chips of ice.

"You want to know the real me, Angel? Fine. Here you go—my mission…" His words faltered a moment before continuing. "My mission was to retrieve something from… Lad's home. And from the tea factory if possible." *A byproduct of the saol-making process*, he continued mind to mind. *Very potent stuff, that crystal powder. Highly addictive.*

S. I gasped.

The base of the S formula, yes. Our scientists have taken it and perverted it into something else entirely. So now you see… I am *like my father. I'm as instrumental as he is in the drug epidemic.*

I shook my head in disbelief. My brain was spinning like a rickety parking-lot-carnival ride. My heartbeat thrummed in my throat. "Did you know?" He couldn't have. Culley *couldn't* have willingly participated in this.

"Know what? What he'd do with it? It doesn't really matter, does it? I knew he couldn't want it for a *good* purpose. I did what he asked, as always. And now it's done. The snowball is rolling downhill, and nothing's going to stop it. You should get out of here, because this entire city— every city—is going to go to shit—fast." *You haven't seen people on S, but I have, every night, in every club I go to. It's wicked stuff, love.* "You're not tough enough to survive what's coming."

"And you are?" I choked on the words, trying to contain my sobs. I'd been worried about Culley being lured in by the seductive club drug, when all the while he was responsible for its creation. It was nearly impossible to believe, but yet the admission had come from his own mouth.

He gave me a resolute stare. "Never doubt it, love. I *am* my father's son."

"No," I said aloud. "There's one difference." Silently I continued. *You care for me. I know it. And if you can love, you can change. You can forgive yourself and move on from the mistakes you've made.*

He met my wet eyes evenly when he replied. "Even if that were true, it wouldn't matter. Good-bye Ava." Ripping his gaze away, he turned to Asher, pinning him with a hard look. "Get her out of here. Today."

Asher nodded. "I will."

Culley strode away and within seconds had disappeared in the crowd. I sucked in a breath, trying to accept what I knew was true—I'd never see him again.

And then I turned to the boy I'd been longing to see every day since I'd left him standing on a sidewalk in Deep River, Mississippi. "I guess we should go."

CHAPTER NINETEEN
HERO MATERIAL

Asher nosed the front of his huge pickup truck out of the garage and into the bumper to bumper traffic.

"So, what was all that about? 'Missions' and stuff? I thought the guy was a model, but he was talking like a soldier or something."

He glanced over at me, waiting for an answer. Which I couldn't give him.

"Um… there are things I'm… not allowed to talk about."

He nodded, a rueful grin crossing his face. "Great. I'm involved with a girl whose ex is special ops. I'm totally going to get knifed in my sleep. He *is* still your ex, right?"

"Yes. And you don't have to worry about him. He made it pretty clear we had his blessing to leave town together." Thinking of Culley's confession and the way he'd practically shoved me into Asher's arms caused a dull ache to spread through my chest. What was he thinking? Why was he helping his father *now* after telling me he'd spent his life trying to avoid him? What would happen to him if he stayed in the Dark Court?

"That's what he *said.*" Asher's tone told me he doubted Culley's resolve.

Though it felt like we made it only inches every half hour, we eventually reached the highway access ramp. Which Asher ignored completely.

"What are you doing? Route 495 is that way."

"Yeah I know." He glanced over and raised one brow. "That's why I'm going *this* way. No matter what he said, I don't trust your special ops pretty boy ex-fiancé as far as I can throw him. If he says we should go 95 South, we're going anything *but* that way. There's plenty of ways to get out of this city. And once we do, we're going to take 81 South, make our way through Maryland and Virginia and Tennessee. That is, if it's okay with you."

I shrugged. "It doesn't matter to me. Whatever you want."

"What I want is to see a smile on that pretty face. You okay? You sure you don't want to go by the apartment and get your stuff?"

I shook my head. "I'm sure."

And no, I wasn't okay. Asher was probably right. I thought I could trust Culley, but I didn't want to take any chances—not with Asher's life. If Culley were to change his mind and mention my defection to his father, there could be someone, or many someones, waiting for us at his apartment. Thanks to Audun's stipend I had cash—I could buy a change of clothes and a toothbrush somewhere along the way. Beyond that, I didn't really need anything.

A police car with flashing lights and blaring siren passed us, making me think of the police detective. I wouldn't be paying him a visit either. Would that be a bad thing for him? Put his life at risk? If Audun couldn't make him forget what he knew, would he make the man disappear? I couldn't think about that right now.

I glanced over at the adorable boy who'd driven more than a thousand miles to come and get me, who'd showed up exactly when I needed him and, with no questions asked, was helping me get away from the man who'd surely kill me on sight when he learned I'd defied him—who'd *delight* in killing Asher on sight. I could not allow that. I felt terrible for Detective Ballard, but when it came down to a choice between his life and Asher's, there *was* no choice.

"What are you thinking about so hard over there?" Asher asked.

"About you. Why did you come? How did you know I'd leave with you?"

"I didn't know. I *hoped* you'd want to come with me. I could tell from Ryann's answers to my questions you weren't real happy with your situation up here." He grinned. "I thought you might be having a problem."

"You and your problem-solving. There are lots of people with problems in the world. Why me? Why do you even like me in the first place? I'm a mess."

Asher chuckled. "Show me one person who *isn't* a mess, and I'll show you a good liar." He paused for a moment, rolling his lips in and back out as if deciding whether to say something. "You know, when I met you, my girlfriend had broken up with me a few days earlier. I'd been walking around in kind of a fog since, and then I saw your car in the Food Star lot there, and the California plates. I'd always wanted to go to California—to go *anywhere* exciting—I knew I had to meet you."

I laughed. "So it was my *license plate* you were interested in."

"At first. And the Corvette. And then you rolled down the window, and I got a look at what was *inside* the Corvette." He stretched out his arm and lay his hand on the seat face up in a clear invitation. I placed my hand on top of his palm. He wrapped his strong fingers around it. "You were so pretty I could hardly breathe looking at you. And you looked so sad. Why were you cryin' that day?"

"It's a long story. I was talking to my mom on the phone. And thinking about my dad."

"Divorced, huh?"

"No… he's dead. He died when I was little."

His fingers squeezed mine. "I'm sorry."

"Thank you." I paused but decided to go ahead and ask the question burning in my mind. "Why did she break up with you?"

"She said she needed a hero. And that I wasn't hero material."

I let out a sharp laugh. "That's ridiculous. I've never met anyone *more* heroic in my life."

He shrugged. "Not really. She said she needed someone who was ready to commit, to be there for her forever. I was… not really ready for all that, and she could tell. Katelynn broke up with me after I finally manned up and was honest with her."

My insides tightened at the statement. What truth had he told that would make his girlfriend break up with him? "About what?"

"I told her I wouldn't be sticking around after graduation. She never wants to leave Deep River. It was kind of a deal breaker."

"Oh. I thought you liked it there. You seem like you're the mayor of that little town or something."

He waved a hand through the air in a dismissive gesture. "It's not that hard to know everyone when there aren't that many people to know. I mean, it's a great town, the people are great, but you know, I want to *do something* with my life."

"Wouldn't you miss the farm? And your family?"

Now he slid a questioning look over at me. "If I didn't know any better, I'd say you're trying to change my mind about getting out of there. I would have thought a big-city girl like you would look down your nose at a nowhere hick town in Mississippi."

"Not at all. I loved it there. It's… cozy." I didn't mention my fetish for land and growing things. This wasn't going to be one of those soul-baring road trips. This was going to be a get-me-to-the-Light-Court-so-I-can-report-back-and-then-get-lost kind of trips. "I think you're lucky to have grown up in a place like that, with people like that."

Asher laughed and shook his head. "You are one weird chick, you know that?"

My laughter joined his. "You have no idea. Hey, how's your granddaddy doing—you know—after the explosion?"

"He's good. Tough old goat. They kept him in the hospital a couple of days after his concussion because of his age, but then I think the nurses were probably begging for mercy, and they sent him home. He's got a limp where he took a piece of stained glass to the knee, but he's already back out working the farm." He gave me a mischievous grin. "He's dying to meet *you*—told him and Momma all about you."

"Oh, you did, huh?" I wouldn't be meeting his family. For some reason the thought made me sad. "I'm sure they were *super*-impressed with my tower-climbing skills."

"Well, maybe I didn't tell them *everything* about you. But I told them you're special—especially to me." Asher cast a long look over at me. His smile was so sweet it was like tiny invisible hook lines had been thrown at my heart and were busily reeling in their catch.

For a long moment I stared at him, filled with a sense of wonder. What was going on here? Was I swaying him unintentionally? I didn't think so. Or maybe this was how it worked—you met someone, and the connection defied all reason. Never having been in a real relationship I couldn't say.

"I don't understand this," I murmured, more to myself than to Asher.

He let out a deep laugh, reaching over to caress my cheek. "Me either. But I'm going with it anyway."

Chapter Twenty
Backstage Access

Asher stuck to his plan of keeping to the back roads. We made our way through Pennsylvania, Maryland, and into Virginia, watching the rocky hills and rolling pastures turn into long stretches of green mountainous terrain as we listened to the radio and talked about anything and everything that came to mind.

He told me about his life, how he loved sports but had stopped playing football, basketball, and baseball in tenth grade because his mom and granddaddy needed his help on the farm, how he loved Marvel movies and vanilla shakes and hated cold weather and sitcoms. How he planned to live in a high rise in a giant city someday and make enough money to have a second home on a beach somewhere.

"You seem older than eighteen to me," I said.

"Well, I've been working on the farm since I was twelve. It's a lot of responsibility. Granddaddy says a heavy load makes a strong man."

Sneaking a glimpse at the large, tanned hands gripping the steering wheel and the muscular arms attached to them, I had to agree. He was curious about my life, too, and I shared as much as I dared about my modeling career and growing up in New York and California.

"It's nice there for sure," I said. "But there's so much natural beauty here." I sighed, staring out the window at the rolling hills and non-stop greenery.

Asher chuckled. "I guess it's true what they say—we always want what we don't have. Here you are, all ga-ga over the sticks while I'm dreaming of getting the hell out of them."

"It's not all it's cracked up to be, you know? City living—it can be lonely. And without someone to share it with, lots of money means nothing."

"Yeah, I figured you for a rich girl—fancy car, fancy clothes. Plus... only rich people say money means nothing."

"It's true—if money could buy happiness, my mom would be the happiest person on earth. She's bought it all at one time or another, and she's *still* miserable."

"Is that why you're running away?"

My head snapped over to face him. "I'm not running away."

"Aww now, don't lie to your old friend, Asher. You're pretty eager to get away from *something*, or I wouldn't be lucky enough to have you here in the cab of my truck.

Maybe it's not your mom, then. Maybe it's your ex-fiancé? I assume this is not just some lovers' spat?"

"No. It's over with him—for good. And no, it's not him I'm running away from exactly. I… it's complicated. I can't really explain it."

I couldn't tell him about Audun and the Dark Court and its plot against the human race—all of it was strictly forbidden to discuss with a human, and it was too dangerous for him to know anyway. Besides, if I did tell him about the Fae world, he'd think I was lying. Or insane.

I felt bad—he'd been so kind to me. I didn't like deceiving him about who I really was and what I was really doing here. It was like a reverse picture of the road trip I'd shared with Culley, when I'd been so angry with him for not being completely honest with me. Now here I was, treating Asher the same way. Was that what Culley had been doing all along—protecting me? It didn't matter. He'd sent me away. I'd never see him again, and I didn't want to—not after what he'd admitted to.

"I think you *could* explain it, but obviously you don't want to. Which is okay—for now. You'll tell me when you're ready." Asher flipped through the radio stations, searching for one that would come in clearly until he landed on a song by Aiden Ray. He put his hands back on the wheel and started nodding his head with the techno-dance beat.

"Ugh." I reached for the buttons to change the station. "I can't stand that little worm."

I'd had to leave New York without confronting him, if he was even *in* the city anymore. Hearing his voice was an unwanted reminder of the things I'd had to do to protect that monster from prosecution.

"Hold on," Asher said, grabbing my hand. "I kind of like that one."

"I take back every nice thing I've ever said about you," I joked. "Your terrible taste in pop music negates it all."

Asher laughed. "You've never *said* anything nice about me. But now of course, I'll have to assume you've been *thinking* nice things. So I'll let you choose the next song."

"Thank you, I said, attempting once again to change the station. But before my finger reached the button, the song ended, and the DJ's voice came on.

"That was Aiden Ray's latest hit 'Mock Me, Make Me.' And I've still got one more pair of tickets for his *sold-out* concert tour to give away to one lucky fan. Be my tenth caller, and you're going to see Aiden *tonight* in concert at the Verizon center in Washington, D.C."

My heart skipped a beat then resumed pumping only now much harder and faster. I turned in my seat to face Asher. "I want to go."

"Go? Go where?"

"To Washington D.C.—to the concert. Tonight."

His face screwed up in a comical scowl. "What? That's at least an hour and a half east of here. We'd barely make it by show time. And we don't have tickets. Besides, I thought you hated the guy."

"I… changed my mind. I need to see him."

Asher blew out a long breath, tilted his head to the side and raised his eyebrows. "Ooookay." He entered the address of the concert venue into his GPS. "What are you planning to do about tickets? Get 'em from a scalper? I hope you really *are* rich, or that's not happening. I didn't bring that much cash."

"Let me worry about getting us in—you just get us there."

"It's a deal," he said and took the exit toward the city.

* * *

We arrived at the Verizon Center about a half hour before the show was scheduled to start. The two closest parking garages we passed had their FULL placards out.

"I have an idea," I said. "Let me out here—I'll see if I can find some tickets, and you can find a place to park. Just come back and meet me out front."

As I climbed out at the curb Asher called, "Hey wait— what's your cell number?"

I told him, and he punched it into his phone so he could call me and make sure we found each other again after he parked.

Oh—my phone. It had come from Audun. I shouldn't be using it anymore. I probably shouldn't even have it *on* me. No doubt Audun could use it to track me down, which he'd surely do when he found out I'd skipped town without doing the job he'd assigned me. Maybe he already knew. That thought scared me—for myself, but more so for Asher. I definitely didn't want *him* calling this number. That would tie him to me and put him on Audun's radar. I had to destroy this phone—now.

It was easy enough to do. I went to the curb and tossed it into the street and waited approximately five minutes. At least four cars rolled directly over it, leaving the phone in pieces strewn across the pavement.

Was it enough? Now that I thought about it, it might be wisest to separate from Asher *now*. I'd have to leave him eventually. This was probably the perfect time and place for it, before we got any more involved.

Except… he'd worry about me. If I disappeared, he'd be sure I'd been kidnapped and go to the police. He'd search for me himself and feel guilty he'd left me alone. He'd be convinced that stupid girl who'd broken up with him and told him he wasn't hero material was right. No. I couldn't do that to him. Audun wasn't aware of Asher's existence, and for now, we were both safe.

I headed toward the entrance of the arena, not bothering with the scalpers waving tickets in my face. My plan was to find Aiden, do what I'd come to do, and get out of here. I wouldn't need a ticket—scalped or otherwise—for that. He'd be waiting in the green room backstage. Having grown up the daughter of an entertainment attorney, I'd been to my share of concerts and had my share of backstage access. I'd never been to this particular arena, but the setup at these places was usually pretty similar.

Getting past the ticket-taker was easy—a bit of Sway while I pretended to dig around in my purse for a lost ticket, and he waved me through. Then I made my way to the VIP area. The corridor to get there, was of course, roped off.

"Hey—hey there—you. You can't go in there." A beefy bodyguard moved toward me as I ducked under the rope.

"It's okay," I called back to him. "I'm with Aiden."

Naturally, the guy chased me down. More Sway. And to the green room I went. Finding it, I encountered a couple more bodyguards, dispatched them, and went inside.

Aiden was alone in the room, scarfing down corn chips by the fistful. His eyes flew open at the sight of me.

"Pre-show energy?" I asked in a flirty tone. I was still wearing my commercial shoot wardrobe and makeup from this morning, so maybe I didn't look *too* different from the girls who no doubt showed up backstage at his shows. Of course, if his tastes ran to fourteen year olds, I was about five years too old for him.

He stood up and smiled. "Oh yeah. Carb-loading. Who are you? Did Raul send you back?"

I smiled and nodded as the singer moved toward me wearing a lusty, expectant expression. So... a girl—or girls—coming back to the green room before the show wasn't unheard of. I wondered who Raul was. An assistant I guessed. Or a pimp.

He took my hand and led me toward a leather couch. "Why don't you come over here? Wow, you're pretty. Are you a model?"

"Yes," I answered honestly. *I'm also your worst nightmare.*

I needed skin-to-skin contact for my glamour to work on him, so I allowed Aiden to keep holding my hand. That quickly turned into rubbing my arm then my shoulder and neck. I'd need to work fast if I wanted to avoid a full-body Swedish massage from this handsy little creep.

"Aiden… how do you remember all those words to all your songs?" I cooed.

He gave me a tolerant I'm-just-humoring-you-to-get-in-your-pants smile. "It's not so hard. I rehearse a lot, and I wrote some of them. Now I have a question for *you*… what have you got on under that dress?" His hand on my leg slid upward.

I gave him a tolerant I'm-just-humoring-you-to-get-in-your-brain smile as I gripped his wrist, stopping him. "You'll never know." And now I turned up my glamour full-steam. "And you'll never be able to remember your lyrics either—ever again—to *any* of your songs, old or new. Every time you get up on stage or in the recording studio, your mind will go blank."

"Wh… what?" His eyes were glazed, his forehead knitted into worry lines.

"Here's what you *will* remember. Every girl you've taken advantage of. Every woman you've forced yourself on when she'd had too much to drink or after she said 'no.' Remember Crystal in New York City? Yeah. That's right. I know about her. I bet you thought you were going to get away with that one when you wrote a big check to the Maggios. *Wrong.* It's going to haunt you day and night until you turn yourself in and get some counseling. You'll be lucky if you can even look at a woman without being overwhelmed with guilt for what a scumbag you've been."

Plucking his dead-weight arm off my shoulder and dropping it to the couch cushion, I stood and faced him. "Okay, we're all done here." Then I nearly skipped toward the door, feeling a hundred pounds lighter. Before leaving, I looked back over my shoulder for a parting shot. "Have a great show tonight."

I couldn't wipe the smile off my face as I headed for the arena's Exit signs. It was almost too bad we wouldn't be hanging around for the show—it was sure to be *entertaining*. But that wouldn't be smart. After leaving the building, I had another moment of indecision. Asher wasn't here yet. I could still walk away. I probably *should* walk away.

But I don't want to.

And then I spotted him coming toward me down the sidewalk. When he caught sight of me, a wide smile overtook his face and he picked up his pace, jogging the last few feet to close the distance between us.

"Hey—I finally found a spot. I'm sorry it took so long."

"Don't worry about it," I said. Feigning disappointment I told him, "I'm sorry, too. I wasn't able to get tickets."

Asher's brows pulled together in obvious confusion as he looked around, noticing several scalpers still hoping for some last minute takers.

I took his hand. "Let's just hit the road, okay? I was right the first time—he *is* a little worm."

"Uh… okay." Asher ran a hand down his face and blew out a breath. "Well, you wait here, and I'll go get the truck. I'll be right back to pick you up."

Squeezing his hand, I pulled him toward the sidewalk. "No, let's walk together. These are comfortable shoes."

He smiled at me. "Okay." Pulling his phone out of his pocket, he looked at it as we walked. "Hey—what was your number again? I think I must have put it in wrong. I called, but you didn't answer."

"Oh—I must have lost it. It's not in my purse anymore."

"Wow, girl, you are murder on cell phones, aren't you?"

I grinned at him and then glanced out at the street where tiny shards of my shattered screen caught the light. Better the phone than us.

CHAPTER TWENTY-ONE
ALWAYS PREPARED

By the time we left the city and got back on the highway it was late. I wasn't tired, but Asher had started yawning and stretching his neck side to side, obviously working out soreness from sitting in one position for too long.

"Tired?" I asked.

"A little. I thought we'd stop before too long. We can't make it all the way back home in one trip—well, I did it on the way up, but it wasn't fun."

"I'm sorry I made us take that stupid side-trip. It added about three hours onto our drive, didn't it? We don't need to stop though. I'll drive."

I did *not* want to stop at any of the hotels along the way—not after realizing my phone could've been tracked to D.C. If Audun had sent someone to tail me, they'd be checking those places. Now that I'd had a chance to think about it, it had probably been very stupid to ever use the phone at all. I had called Ryann and Lad on it.

"What's the matter? Don't trust me?" Asher teased. "We can get separate rooms, but I'm too wiped out to jump your bones anyway."

"No... I..." Could I confide my fears to him? Since he was driving me, he might be in danger, too. It seemed only fair to tell him at least what I *could* about my situation. "I don't want to stop at a hotel. I'm worried we won't be safe. We might have been followed."

His usually cheery expression fell into a mask of concern. "What's going on, Ava? Who's following you? Your ex? 'Cause I can handle him."

"No. No, it's not like that." Although now that I thought about it, who else would Audun assign to follow me? Culley would know exactly where I'd gone. Now I was even more certain we couldn't stop at any hotels along the way. "It's... his father I'm worried about. He's very powerful, and he thinks I owe him something."

"Money?"

"My allegiance."

Asher was quiet for a few minutes. Then he ventured an educated guess. "Is he in the mafia or something?"

"Something like that," I said quietly. The Runes *were* a powerful family. And participating in organized crime, now that I thought about it. "He's kind of a drug dealer, and I don't want any part of it. Have you heard about S?"

"Yeah. I was listening to NPR on the way to New York. That stuff is bad news. If he's into that, you're smart to get far away from him. Do you think he might be following you because he's afraid you'll talk?"

"Among other reasons."

"No problem then. We'll keep going. I'm fine."

Another hour into the trip and Asher's eyelids started drooping. Once he even drifted to the side until the truck's big tires came into contact with that bumpy strip of textured pavement in the breakdown lane. He jerked the wheel back, straightening the truck out again. "Sorry."

"Please let me drive," I said. But honestly, I was starting to doze myself, and the noise and vibrations had startled me awake, too. I yawned, looking around. "Where do you think we are?"

Just then a billboard came into view.

"Shenandoah National Park," Asher said, reading it. His tone brightened. "I have an idea." He followed the sign's suggestion and took the exit for I-66.

"What are you doing? I thought you understood—we can't stop at a hotel."

"We're not," he said. "Trust me."

The highway wound through a dark, hilly area for about seven miles before Asher slowed the truck. Outside the window I read a low, dark sign with white lettering.

Entering Shenandoah National Park

"Are we sightseeing?" I joked. It was pitch black dark without even a streetlight to be seen for miles.

Asher grinned. "You, city girl, are going camping."

"Camping? How can we go camping? What—do you have camping gear in the back of your truck? You do, don't you?"

He nodded. "See? What did I tell you? I'm an expert at solving problems."

"Are you a Boy Scout or something?"

"No, but I *am* always prepared." Smiling over at my open-mouthed shock, he explained. "Look, I like camping, okay? I went last weekend with my buddy Richie. We did some fishing, target shooting… you know?"

I just shook my head. I'd *never* known anyone like him. Of course I hadn't actually known *any* humans very well, but surely they couldn't all be as smart and capable and utterly adorable as this one.

"Okay then, what do we do? Find a campsite?" I found myself whispering as we continued into the dark park.

He shook his head. "It's too late. The registration office will be closed by now, and they've probably booked up all the sites anyway. We're going backwoods camping. It's always open and always free at these parks."

I wasn't too sure I liked the sound of that. "What's backwoods camping?"

He laughed at my suspicious tone and expression. "Don't worry—nothing scary. It means there are no trash facilities or bath houses close by."

"Sounds pretty scary to me," I muttered.

He chuckled. "I think being followed by drug dealers sounds scarier, but you didn't even mention it until we were four hours into this thing."

"You're right. I wasn't thinking. I'm sorry I got you into this. If you want to just drop me off at the next city we come to—"

"Oh yeah." His voice was filled with angry sarcasm as he pulled the truck into a spot and parked it. "I'm just going to leave you stranded in the middle of Virginia. Is that what you think of me—that I'd abandon you? Now you sound like Katelynn."

"No. No Asher. I don't think that. I think you're the nicest, most generous, most... incredible guy I've ever met. I was only..."

His smile returned. "That's okay. You can stop there." He pulled the keys from the ignition. "Wait in here if you want while I get everything we'll need. It might be kind of chilly out there now that we're at a higher elevation."

"No, I'll help you." I slid out of the truck and joined him at the tailgate as he removed the bed-topper and unpacked some very neatly stored camping gear. I shivered with cold. "You really are prepared, aren't you?"

He grinned down at me, tugging off his jacket and placing it on my shoulders before slipping a large backpack over his arms one at a time. "For anything. How 'bout you, city girl?"

I couldn't help myself—I giggled for the first time since I was a child, snuggling into the jacket that was still warm from his body heat and carried his enticing scent. Who was this guy and why did I react to him like this? It was crazy. I was crazy. I knew that for a fact since I was at that very moment walking into the dark forest *on purpose* with the intention of spending the night *outdoors*.

Flashlight in hand and holding a couple of lightweight bags Asher finally agreed to let me carry, I followed him. "How will you know when we've found a good spot?"

"I'll know it when I know it," he said.

"Okay then. Lead on, mountain man."

Finally he announced we'd found the place. I wasn't sure how he could tell it from the acres of dark woods we'd already hiked through but I didn't argue.

"Can you hold this?" Asher gave me easy tasks to do while he did the heavy lifting of setting up the campsite by the light of a battery-operated lantern.

He was so fast and efficient I couldn't help but be impressed—not to mention the absorbing show his muscles put on as he lifted and squatted, gripped and pressed and twisted and reached. It was like some kind of one-man exotic male revue, only with slightly more clothing and fewer spotlights. Anyone who could make backwoods camping look sexy had some serious game.

"All right. Home sweet home," Asher announced, then turned around to look at me. "Hey, you okay? You're real quiet back there."

"Sure. I'm fine." I made my way to the small tent on shaky legs. Did I mention how small the tent was? And I was supposed to sleep in there *with* him? After watching *that*?

As I reached Asher at the tent entrance, he put a reassuring hand on my shoulder. Well, it was probably meant to be reassuring. Instead it sent a bolt of electricity through my body as if I'd been plugged into a giant charger. I balked at climbing inside, my breathing erratic, my heart chasing its own beats trying to catch up.

Asher's voice was low and calming. "There's no reason to be scared, Ava. We're safe out here. The black bears in these parts are really shy of humans."

"Bears?" I yelped and scooted into the tent.

Asher crawled in behind me, chuckling to himself. The inside of the tent felt close but not claustrophobic. The walls slanted in toward us. The floor of it was surprisingly comfortable, as if it was resting on a patch of grass—it probably was since Asher had picked the spot. I hadn't been able to see the area very well and hadn't paid strict attention to the ground. Directly in the center of the tent, stretching from one end to the other, was a sleeping bag. *A* sleeping bag.

"There's... only one," I said.

"Yeah, sorry about that, but I only have the one. Richie brought his own last weekend. Not that I would have shared with him. Now when it comes to you—I don't mind sharing a bit." He gave me a big grin.

I rolled my eyes. "So generous."

"That's the kind of guy I am. No seriously, it's better anyway—for heat purposes. It's gonna get cold tonight, and you don't have the right clothes on."

I was still in my ring commercial dress. I'd borrowed Asher's jacket for the hike here, but my legs were bare, and I had no socks on—just the flats I'd worn for the shoot.

"Okay." The reluctance was obvious in my tone, but what was I going to do? Hike back to the truck—with the *bears*? No way. I'd take my chances with the *domesticated* animal in front of me.

As if reading my mind, Asher said, "Don't worry. I'll be a perfect gentleman. Promise. You hungry?"

Suddenly my stomach remembered it was there and answered him with a loud growl. Asher laughed. "Watch out there—the bears are gonna be scared of *you* with all that racket."

"Very funny."

He produced two protein bars and some bottled water. "You get started on this, and I'll make us some soup real quick."

"You have soup?" Soup had never sounded so appealing in my life.

Asher backed out of the tent, and I watched through the open flap as he retrieved a small gas burner from his backpack and set a pot on it. Then he pulled out two cans of soup and a can opener. Squatting, he opened and emptied the cans then stirred. The sound of a slow boil reached my ears as the smell of hot food teased my nostrils. A few minutes later he gestured for me to come out and join him. Lured by the scent, I did.

"Here—have a seat."

Asher dragged a log over for me to sit on. Kneeling in front of me, he dipped a spoon into the pot, lifted it and blew on it, and then took a taste before holding it up to my lips. "It's just right—not too hot not too cold."

I smirked. "In case you hadn't noticed, my locks are red, not gold."

"Oh, I noticed all right. As soon as you rolled that little Corvette window down. I saw that red hair, and I was a goner."

I hoped it was too dark for him to see my blush. My face felt about fifty degrees hotter than the air around us. There was no way the temperature of the campfire soup could come close. I let him feed me a spoonful then reached for the utensil.

"I can do this, you know."

"I don't want you to burn your hand reaching into the pot. Let me. We don't have any bowls or I'd let you feed yourself. Maybe. I kind of like this." Blowing on another spoonful, he offered it to me. "Open up."

Starvation won out over embarrassment. I opened my mouth. But as the spoon-feeding went on, alternating between me and him, and the volume in the pot got lower, my body kept on heating up. Maybe it was the way Asher's eyes sparked as he looked at me, or the slow smile that spread across his face as he watched me sip and swallow. It was just soup but it was also… sexy.

At one point it became too much. His eyes locked with mine as his hand inched the spoon slowly toward my mouth. He touched the tip of the spoon to my lower lip, opening it, then pulled away, brought it back and teased my lips apart again. His breathing was audible and fast in the quiet night.

I pulled back without taking the bite. "Um… that's enough for me, I think. You finish it."

Asher blinked and straightened his legs, standing and backing away to let me move past him toward the refuge of the tent. "Sure. I'll uh… see you in there. In a minute."

I ducked into the opening flap and collapsed onto the sleeping bag, squeezing my eyes shut and willing my heart to stop racing. Outside the tent I heard the sounds of Asher cleaning up the dinnerware. And then the flap opened again, and he entered the tent, turning awkwardly in the small space to zip it closed behind him.

"What about the bears?" I asked, revealing my newest terror. "Won't they smell the food and come investigate?"

"I doubt they'll even come around. I washed everything and put the dishes and our other supplies in a bag that I strung up in a tree. Even if they do come snooping, there's no food in here, so you have nothing to worry about tonight." He hesitated then continued. "Unless…"

"What? Unless what?"

"Well, unless one of them has a sweet tooth. There's an awfully sweet girl in here." His hands came to my ribcage, and he tickled me mercilessly, laughing as I shrieked and giggled and begged him to stop.

"I'll have to growl at them, and show them my teeth, and tell them this is *my* delicious strawberry cupcake, and I'm not sharing," he said.

"Enough, enough," I wheezed. "I can't take any more."

When he ended the tickle-torture and I stopped thrashing, I realized our legs were tangled and I was in

Asher's arms, nose to nose with him. His breath hit my face in hot rapid strikes that matched my own accelerated breathing.

"You sure about that?" he whispered against my lips. "I think you can take…" His mouth inched closer. "… a little… more."

And then his lips pressed against mine, and my racing heart worked even faster, and the breathlessness increased until I thought I might pass out. At least I was already lying down.

Asher kissed me harder, and God help me, I let him.

CHAPTER TWENTY-TWO
YES AND NO

What are you doing Ava? This is wrong. It's insane. You can't do this. You can't fall for this guy.

That's what was going on in my brain.

My body? Different story. My leg that was wrapped around Asher's wrapped itself tighter. My arm that had been flailing to escape him moments earlier went up and around his neck, and my fingers sank into his smooth, soft hair, loving the cool feel of it, loving the warmth underneath.

Feeling my response to him, Asher yanked me closer with a low growl that might actually have been enough to frighten a few bears away, but for one nineteen-year-old Elven virgin it only heightened the excitement. Holding me tight against him, he rolled onto his back, then rolled again, so I was pinned beneath him, my back pressed into the warm, soft sleeping bag.

It felt amazing to have the weight of him over me, his big, hard body pressed all along mine. Angling his face over mine, he kissed me deeper, communicating his rapidly building desire with every stroke of his tongue.

I'll stop him in a minute, my mind vowed as the minutes ticked by and my body did everything in its power to encourage him to continue. I literally couldn't help myself. The feelings he'd awakened in me were so powerful, so overwhelming, I almost forgot he was human and I was not and we had no business doing even half of what we were doing together.

It was getting warm in the tiny tent. Asher must have felt it too, because he raised up on an elbow and yanked off his t-shirt in one quick move. *Holy Cow.* The air rushed out of my lungs at the sight of him shirtless.

I ran my fingers greedily over his chest and down to his fascinating abdominal muscles. *Oh yes.* They felt every bit as good as they looked. Better than anything. Obviously taking my greedy touches as encouragement, Asher dropped his persuasive mouth to my neck, spreading hot kisses over it as his hand slid to my back and eased the zipper of my dress down. *Yes yes yes.* I wanted *out* of this restrictive thing, and I wanted him out of his jeans and anything else that dared to come between us, and *yes* I wanted to feel his skin, all of it, and... oh no.

No no no.

Pressing both palms against his chest, I pushed myself back and stared into Asher's heavy-lidded eyes.

He gave me a sexy pleasure-drunk smile. "You okay? If you're worried about protection, I told you, I'm always prepared for anything."

He reached into his back pocket and drew out his wallet, began opening it.

"No!" I yelped and sat up straight. One shoulder of my unfastened dress slipped down my arm, and I pushed it back into place.

Asher's face contracted in concern. He sat up as well. "What's the matter? Were you not... I thought you wanted..."

"No," I interrupted. "I mean, yes, I did. I do. But we can't. I can't. Not with you." I was nearly in hysterics. What was I doing? What had I done? I was Elven. He was human—one hundred percent—not even a human-Elven hybrid like Ryann, who at least had *some* hope of immortality. And I'd been *so close* to forgetting all that and letting it happen. *It* could *not* happen—not for us.

Dress gaping in the back, I crawled toward the tent door and fumbled for the zipper, planning I guess to walk through the dark forest to the highway, or maybe to ask a willing bear to put me out of my misery.

Asher's gentle hand on my shoulder stopped me. "Ava stop. Wait. Turn around please and look at me."

"I can't." The tears started and would not stop. I gave up on the maddening zipper and let my face fall into my hands, trying to escape Asher's watchful eyes.

He rubbed my back as I cried, murmuring, "It's okay. Everything's okay." After a few minutes, he pulled me back into a sitting position on the sleeping bag. "Can you look at me now? Can you tell me what's going on?"

I did open my eyes and take in his troubled expression. "I can't. I *can't* tell you."

"Okay, okay. That's fine. What if I guess it? Would you tell me if I'm right or wrong?"

I shook my head. "You'll never guess."

"Did somebody hurt you, Ava? Assault you? Was it your ex?"

Stunned for a moment by his assumption, I stopped crying abruptly. "No. He… he didn't do anything to me. He'd never do that."

"Someone else then?"

"No. No one assaulted me. I…" I let out a shaky breath and drew a new one, clenching my eyelids closed. This was horrible. I'd acted bizarrely, and now Asher was upset. All he'd done was make me feel good, better than I'd ever felt in my whole life, and I had flipped out. Now he was convinced I'd been the victim of some terrible thing. Ugh. I wanted to be invisible. I wanted to sink into the ground under the moss and pine needles. I did *not* want to say what I had to say. But he deserved the truth. At least some of it.

"I'm a virgin," I blurted. Then before I could chicken out, I spilled the rest of it in a brisk stream-of-consciousness ramble. "I mean like a *virgin* virgin—I haven't done *anything*. With *anyone*. Ever. I don't know what I'm doing, and I didn't really think about what was happening because it was all so fast, and it felt so good, and you're so good at it, and you're so good looking, and then I panicked because

I can't let it happen, but I wanted to, and I was about to anyway, but I can't, and now you must think I'm a horrible tease—"

Asher took my hands in his and rubbed his thumbs gently over my knuckles. "Okay, I think I get it." There was laughter in his voice but he did not laugh. "It's okay. I understand. We'll go slow. We'll wait till you're ready."

I stared at him in shock. He wasn't angry. He didn't seem to think I was crazy. Or a horrible tease. The problem was, no matter how great Asher was—and he was pretty great—I could never tell him what *I* actually *was.*

"What if I'm never ready?" I asked in a small voice.

He gave me a slow grin, deepening his massage of my hands. "You will be. And I can be very patient when I want something enough."

There was no doubt in his voice at all. None in his eyes. Just a searing heat that told me he still wanted me and a self-confidence that stunned me. I'd never met anyone like him. I doubted I ever would again.

"Now come here and let me zip up your dress, and then we're going to get into this sleeping bag, and you're going to let me hold you, and we're going to get some sleep. As my granddaddy always says, 'Lay your head with the dark, you'll raise it with the lark.'"

I couldn't help it—I laughed. I scooted in beside him, and he tucked me against his side, my face resting comfortably in the nook between his shoulder and chest. And just like that, everything was okay again.

Well, not everything. I was falling hard for a human boy I had no business even being with. I was *way* too attracted to him, and I had a feeling that given the smallest bit of encouragement, he'd have me breathing heavy and desperate for his touch again.

Already, just lying beside him with my head on his chest, I felt my body responding to his nearness. I listened to his heart beat its slow, steady rhythm as he fell asleep, thinking of his kisses, of the way his hands felt on my skin. *Oh boy.* I scooted away from his body. I wasn't going to be able to handle this. I wasn't going to be able to be around Asher and *not* want to kiss him and touch him and do *it.*

Being careful not to wake him, I unzipped my side of the sleeping bag and slipped out of it, moving toward the doorway. There must have been a bright moon because it wasn't completely dark in the tent. I could see the rise and fall of his chest and the shape of his face—the strong forehead and straight nose, the full lips, and the jaw that even now I longed to run my fingertips along.

He was beautiful. He was kind. He was strong.

And he was determined to help me. And *wait* for me. Ugh.

If I managed to sneak away tonight, he'd probably look for me. Strike that *probably*—he'd definitely look for me. He might keep looking for me long past the time he should return home and go back to school, back to his family, back to his life. He'd feel responsible and... sad. I didn't want that.

No, the best thing for Asher would be for me to wake him up and use my glamour on him, to make him forget all about me. I'd convince him he'd gone on a solo adventure up to New York City and then to this park, fulfilled some of that wanderlust he'd told me about. Maybe it would even help him feel better about what he thought of as his "small," "boring" life in Deep River.

I placed my hand on his bare arm, and he stirred. I'd start the process immediately, as soon as he was conscious, before he even got the chance to say something that might change my mind. This was hard enough as it was. The thought of leaving him made my heart heavy, and my eyes were already swimming with tears.

"Ava? Sweetie?" Asher lifted his head. His sleep-roughened voice brushed softly over my ears. "What is it?"

This was it. It was time.

"I…" The words wouldn't come out. They were stuck there in my throat, struggling to move past the huge lump that had formed there.

"Ava?" he asked again.

"It's nothing," I whispered. "I had a bad dream."

Both of his arms reached out to me. "Come on back to bed. I'll make it better."

Letting out the breath I'd been holding, I followed his instructions, curling up once more by his side, where it *was* better somehow. I closed my eyes and let my muscles relax, feeling guilty and relieved at the same time.

Tomorrow. I'd do it then, and then I'd leave him. For tonight, I allowed myself to snuggle close against his warm strength and dream this was how it would always be.

Chapter Twenty-Three
Simple Things

I woke to the sound of birds and the smell of… something good.

Extricating myself from the sleeping bag, I crawled to the tent flap and unzipped it. Asher was outside, sitting on the log in front of the small burner, cooking.

"Is that bacon?"

He turned his head and saw me. "Well good morning. It's turkey bacon—I didn't get my Thanksgiving turkey yesterday, and this was the closest thing I could find. You hungry?"

I nodded and climbed out of the tent. "Starved. Where on earth did you get that—not from the bed of your truck?"

He laughed. "No. I'm prepared, but I don't travel with a full grocery store. I walked over to the campground store and picked up some stuff for breakfast. You want coffee?"

He reached down by his foot and grabbed a white lidded cup, lifting it in my direction.

"Oh *yes*." I took the hot beverage gratefully, inhaling the steam rising from the lid's small opening. "I can't believe I didn't wake up when you left. What time is it?"

"About seven. You were pretty tired I guess. You were up some during the night with bad dreams—remember? Here—I got muffins, too."

I nodded, accepting the paper bag and peeking inside. I did remember. I remembered coming very close to glamouring away his memories of me last night. This morning I was glad I hadn't done it.

Seeing him sitting there shirtless, cooking for me, with a backdrop of sun-dappled leaves and a small stream trickling in the background was a memory *I* wouldn't have wanted to miss out on. Now it was mine to keep forever, to add to the collection of moments with him that became more valuable to me all the time. Spending the night in his arms was easily at the top of the list so far, though Asher had an amazing ability to top himself when it came to impressing me.

Maybe we could just have this one more day. He'd told me the drive to Mississippi would take another twelve hours. I needed to get there anyway. I needed to inform Lad and Ryann of what Audun was up to. After that, maybe I'd stay in Altum a night or two and regroup, come up with a plan for the rest of my life.

"So… what do you want to do today?" Asher asked.

I finished chewing my bite of blueberry muffin. "What do you mean? We're driving, aren't we?"

"Yes, but I thought we might take a hike first. If anyone was following you, they've gone long past us now, or they're still busy checking out every hotel along the highway between here and Knoxville. I picked up a park map at the store. There's a big waterfall not too far from our campsite. And over in Luray there's a giant cavern full of stalactites and stalagmites, if you're interested. We'd have to drive there, but it would probably be worth it. I'll bet you've never seen anything like it."

I swallowed a laugh. I could show him a cavern that would knock his little human socks off—and it was about five miles outside his hometown in Mississippi. "The hike to the waterfall sounds nice but we should probably hit the road after that."

"So *eager* to get back to the boondocks." He shook his head and took a small pill bottle from the bag, removing the cap and tapping a few assorted tablets into his palm. He threw them into his mouth and washed them down with coffee.

"What are those?" I asked. "You're not sick, are you?"

The chilling sensation of alarm was yet another reminder we shouldn't be together. I would never contract a human virus, infection, cancer, or heart disease. I'd live forever unless something violent happened to end my life— which admittedly was a possibility considering my current reckless behavior. But Asher… he was fragile, in spite of his strength. If I decided to give in to this thing, I would eventually lose him. I wasn't sure I could handle that.

"Healthy as a horse." He grinned. "These are supplements—iron, Vitamin D, a multivitamin. Granddaddy got me started on them real young—he's a big believer. He always says, 'Good health is better than muckle wealth.'"

And just like that I was laughing again. It was hard to be morose around Asher. After finishing breakfast and cleaning up we made our way to the closest path and headed for the waterfall he'd spotted on the park map. Because I wasn't really geared up for proper hiking, we stuck to the beaten path.

He was right—Dark Hollow Falls wasn't far away. It would have been worth a long hike, though. Water rushed over an uneven slope of dark, moss-covered rocks, splitting into several separate falls then rejoining in a single stream into a cold, rock-lined pool at the bottom. The entire picture was framed by orange and yellow-leafed trees that reflected in the water.

"Beautiful, isn't it?" Asher looked back over his shoulder at me then resumed taking pictures with his phone.

"It is. Gorgeous."

Cool mist rose off the water and glowed in the morning sun, making the place feel magical. It seemed like an Elven place. Because it was early, we were the only ones there. Taking a seat on a boulder overlooking the water, Asher and I stretched out our legs and enjoyed the view.

"I like this," I said, leaning my head against his shoulder. "I could live here."

"Live here, city girl? That's a bold statement. You do realize there's no Nordstrom or Starbucks around the corner, right?"

"I mean it. Maybe not *here* but somewhere remote, somewhere quiet. It's so peaceful. I don't need Nordstrom or Starbucks. I think the things that really make you happy are the simplest… like the taste of hot coffee in the morning." I held up the cup he'd given me and gestured to the rippling stream. "And the sound of running water, the smell of fresh air."

He nodded, looking thoughtful, no doubt thinking of his own ambitions to leave the simple life behind. "You can have those things in a big city."

"Yes," I agreed. "But they can get lost in all the noise and busyness. And even a city of millions of people can be lonely if you feel like no one really knows you. There's something precious about knowing people—and being known. You have that in Deep River."

"I never thought about it like that before." He laughed. "You almost make me want to stick around that little one-horse town." But his smile disappeared as he worked his fingers under a clump of moss and pried it from the rock. "My dad says only losers stay, live, and die in the town where they were born."

"I've never heard you mention your father before. You've talked about your mom, and you mention your granddaddy all the time, but never your dad."

His expression curdled. He threw the moss into the water and watched it bob and float downstream. "There's not all that much to say. I see him about once or twice a year. He's a decent guy, I guess."

"So your parents are divorced."

"They were never married."

"Oh. Where does he live? In Mississippi?"

"No. Right now he's in Houston, I *think*. He moves around a lot—short attention span." He smirked. "I've always thought it was a pretty cool life, traveling, seeing new places, no responsibilities, nothing to tie you down."

Contrary to his words, his face betrayed how deeply it hurt that his father bothered to see him only a few times a year. He was acting tough, but I *knew*—kids needed their dads. It was bad enough when your father was absent through no fault of his own, like mine. When it was by choice... well, I could only imagine the pain.

I folded my fingers with his and looked directly into his eyes. "He doesn't know what he's missing out on."

The way he held my gaze was so intense, so *intimate*, my heart flipped over in my chest and started mugging my lungs, stealing their oxygen. I pulled my hand away and pretended to stretch.

"So, wanna trade lives? I'll live on the farm in Deep River, and you can take over my place in California—and deal with my mother." I forced a laugh.

Tension broken, Asher laughed, too. He looked up at the sky as if pretending to think about it. "Does this deal come with a Corvette?" Jumping to his feet, he struck a pose on the boulder. "Although I'm not sure how I'd go over as a supermodel." Another silly pose. "What do you think? Next swimsuit edition?"

I pretended to click photos as he rotated through a few more Vogue moves. Then Asher whipped off his shirt—and looked like the real thing. He wasn't Elven, but with his height and wide shoulders and muscular build, he could give most of them a run for their money. Maybe *all* of them. Even Culley's physique didn't appeal to me this much.

I tried to keep my voice casual. "What are you doing?" *Besides making me drool?*

"I'm going in for a quick swim," he said. "Want to come?"

Taking in his bare torso and his hands moving down to the button of his jeans, I ducked my head and got to my feet. "No, you go ahead—it's too cold for me. I need to go to the bathroom before we get on the road anyway. I saw a sign on the trail for one." Keeping my eyes trained on my toes, I headed for the path, making a hasty retreat from the too-tempting sight.

Asher's voice followed me to the trail. "Okay, your loss. I'll catch up to you in a minute."

After visiting the bathhouse and freshening up, I waited at the head of the trail for Asher. He arrived within five minutes, fully clothed thank God, but no less tempting. His cheeks were pink with exhilaration. Against them his eyes looked ultra-blue. His smile was wide and dazzling.

"Now *that* was a cold shower." He shook his head, flinging the remaining water from his short hair. "I feel like a new man. Maybe you're right—maybe it is the simple things in life."

I nodded and fell into step beside him, bracing myself for a twelve hour ride inches away from the most tempting guy I'd ever met.

I'd been right about another thing, too. I was in *trouble* with this guy. As soon as we got back to Deep River, I *had* to erase his memory and get away from him—before *I* forgot everything else that mattered.

CHAPTER TWENTY-FOUR
WE NEVER MET

We made it to town around nine Friday night. Because it was Black Friday, many of the stores on Main Street were still open for pre-Christmas shoppers, and there was a decent amount of traffic on the street.

The Sonic, of course, was jumping. Asher pulled in and parked in one of the diagonal spots, rolling down his window and checking out the lighted menu board. His finger hovered over the red call-button.

"Know what you want?"

"Um... no. I've never eaten here before."

"What? Never been to Sonic? You haven't lived, city girl. Welcome to civilization. I recommend the bacon cheeseburger or the chicken strips. And you've got to have a cherry lime-aid."

I wrinkled my nose. "That sounds gross."

He laughed. "Oh no. You want to be a small town girl, you've got to adapt your palate. Cherry lime-aid is like the champagne of Deep River. And you're going to love it. Trust me, it's delicious."

"Okay then. I'll have one of those. And the chicken strips."

Asher grinned his approval and pushed the button, giving our orders to the squawky voice on the other end.

As we sat and waited for our food, I watched groups of teenagers arrive in their cars, get out, mingle and flirt. Several of the boys looked freshly showered, with wet hair and DRHS football t-shirts on. A girl pointed in our direction, and her friend looked up, wide-eyed with surprise. Then she strutted over and knocked on the hood of Big Red before going to Asher's window.

He rolled it down. "Hey Bon-bon. What's up?"

"Asher McCord—I can't believe you missed the playoff game tonight. Where *were* you?"

Her eyes darted to me, making a quick assessment before returning to Asher's face, where they clearly preferred to focus.

"Out of town. Just got back." He leaned back in his seat. "Bonnie, this is Ava. Ava—Bonnie."

I lifted a hand in a wave. "Hi."

She gave me the least friendly, perfunctory smile I'd ever seen. "Hi." Then back to Asher. "Katelynn was asking about you today. She should be here any minute." She tossed a glance to me. "Katelynn's his girlfriend."

Asher's open expression shut down. "*Ex*-girlfriend. Listen Bon, great to see you, but our food's coming. I'll catch you later."

She blinked and stayed in place for a moment. Then realizing she'd been dismissed, she sniffed and whirled away, heading back toward her friends on the other side of the patio area that centered the two parking lanes. Reaching them, she spoke quickly and enthusiastically, gesturing in our direction. The others turned and stared.

Suddenly feeling conspicuous and very out of place, I looked away from the group and focused on the waitress hooking a tray onto the window of Asher's truck. He paid her, thanked her, then lifted two tall styrofoam cups and offered one to me.

"Your cherry lime-aid, miss. Tell me this isn't Heaven in a cup," he challenged with an adorable smile.

He obviously hadn't noticed Bonnie's live-up-to-the-minute breaking news report across the drive-in or the way the other kids were watching us now. Either that or he didn't care. I did. I couldn't help myself. Under their scrutiny I felt like an alien or a zoo animal trapped in my tiny habitat.

I forced a return smile for Asher and took a sip of the red liquid through my straw, nodding and declaring it good. But in all honesty, it tasted sour. Maybe it wasn't the drink but the discomfort of being a stranger in a new place. Maybe it was the realization that as much as I loved the quaintness of this town and longed to fit in, I never would.

My fantasy of living in a place like this, living in peace, growing my little garden, knowing and being known, was exactly that—a fantasy. I wasn't like Asher's ex-girlfriend. I wasn't like these people. I couldn't be one of them, no matter how much I might want to.

When we'd finished eating, Asher pulled the truck back onto Main Street and headed out of town in the direction of his family's farm. It also happened to be the direction of Altum.

"I can't wait for you to meet Momma and Granddaddy," he said. "They are gonna *love* you."

"Yeah… about that. I think it might have to wait. I need to talk to Ryann. I'm pretty sure I'll just spend the night with her."

His head whipped around in surprise. "Really? They've already got a room ready for you. I called them from the last rest stop we made."

"Oh, that's so sweet. But yeah… I really think it's best if I stay with her tonight."

He shrugged. "Okay, if that's what you want. But your suitcase—you know the one from the trunk of your Corvette? It's already at my house. Momma loves your clothes, by the way." He winked. "She peeked."

"Oh good. I'd actually forgotten about that. I have clothes—yay! So I'll see you tomorrow then… maybe."

"Oh, there's no maybe about it. I'll let you get away from me tonight, reluctantly, but I'll be back to get you tomorrow. You have to come to our annual Pecan Pickin' Party."

I couldn't help but grin, despite the encroaching sadness at the thought of leaving him. "What's that?"

"Well, we have a grove of pecan trees. They line our whole driveway from the county route all the way up to the house. Every year our friends and neighbors come over one Saturday during the season, and we hand out buckets to anyone who wants one. Everybody picks up the pecans that have fallen until their buckets are so heavy they can barely lift them. Then they take them home to eat or bake into pies or whatever."

"I love pecans."

"Me too, which is amazing considering how many I've eaten in my lifetime. It's a wonder I haven't turned into a walking breathing nut."

I laughed and held up a finger before he caught his mistake.

"I guess that's up for debate, huh?" He laughed. "Well, anyway, you're gonna love it. It's a good time. Momma makes homemade bread and pots of chili, and everybody stays and has a meal out on the picnic tables under the trees."

I sighed deeply, picturing the idyllic domestic scene. "It sounds nice."

He grinned and grabbed my hand, bringing my knuckles to his lips for a kiss. "It is. And it'll be even better with you there this year. You'll get to meet pretty much everybody who's important in my life."

Ooof. There went the warm feeling in my middle, replaced instantly by a heavy cold stone. I couldn't go to a

Pecan Picking Party or any other event involving his family and friends. Not if I was going to erase his memories of me and disappear. One snotty little girl at the Sonic was one thing—all the important people in his life—that was another thing entirely.

I was quiet for the rest of our drive out to Ryann's house. My fingers clenched Asher's until he must have wondered what was wrong with me. With every mile closer we drew to the log house in the woods, my heart gained weight. By the time we arrived, it weighed a hundred pounds all by itself. I was struggling to hold back tears. This was it. Our trip was done. I had to say good-bye to him tonight—forever.

The truck rolled down the gravel driveway and around the curve, bringing the house into view. The front porch light was on, and Ryann's new car was there in the circular drive. Asher put the truck into park and reached for the keys as if to turn it off.

"Want me to walk you in?"

I shook my head. "No. I'll just get out here. I don't have any bags or anything to carry in."

"Right." He nodded. Then he turned off the ignition and shifted in his seat to face me. "Well then I guess this is the part where you feel so grateful for the ride home, you give me a mind-erasing goodnight kiss."

Momentarily horrified, my eyes flew open wide. Then I realized he was kidding about the mind-erasing part. Of course. He didn't know about my terrible gift. I stared at him for long, greedy moments, drinking in all the beautiful details of his face.

"I *am* grateful," I whispered. "For everything."

"It was my pleasure," he whispered back.

Then he leaned in and kissed me. His mouth was gentle as it worked over mine, coaxing me to give in to the intoxicating sensations he never failed to evoke. As he deepened the kiss, I sagged against him, filled with pleasure and despair. How was I going to live without this for the rest of my life?

Asher pulled back, keeping eye contact, holding me in place with those incredible turquoise eyes of his.

"Uh oh. It didn't work," he murmured. "There is nothing…" A soft kiss. "…that could *ever*…" Another one. "…make me forget you. Not as long as I live."

His lips met mine one more time before he sat back with a smile then got out to come around and open my door for me. I waited, fighting with all my strength not to cry, dying inside by the minute.

Why, why, *why* was this happening? Why did the universe throw this perfect, amazing guy in my path when there was no way for me to keep him?

I slid from the seat, and Asher's big hands caught me, settling at my waist. Gliding my hands from his wrists up his forearms to his biceps, I relished the feel of his skin under my fingertips this one last time. This was it. I had to do it.

"Asher."

"Yeah?" he said as he stared down into my eyes. His voice was husky, and I could tell from the look he was giving me he was about to kiss me again. I couldn't let that happen. If my heart opened to him even one more inch, I might lose my nerve and not do what I needed to.

Heart pounding in my ears, I swallowed, took a breath, and began. "That day… that day at the grocery store when you saw my car and noticed the license plate… you walked over and knocked on the window…" I paused and took another shaky breath. "… but I didn't roll it down. I backed out of the spot and drove away."

He cocked his head to the side and blinked a couple of times. "What are you…"

I forged ahead, interrupting him. "You never saw me up on the electrical tower. You never pulled me out of my smashed car. When you drove to New York City recently, it was only because you wanted to see the parade and the city. It had nothing to do with me, and you never even saw me there. We didn't make that drive home together. We didn't camp together and sleep in each other's arms last night." I was struggling to even finish sentences toward the end, my voice breaking. "You don't… know me at all. We never met."

For a long moment, he stared at me with a blank expression. Then his eyes narrowed, crinkling at the corners. The sides of his lips raised. "What the *hell* are you talking about, crazy girl? I think that cherry lime-aid went right to your brain and froze something up there." He laughed.

My jaw literally dropped open.

"If you think pleading temporary insanity is going to get you out of meeting my family, think again. I'll be back to pick you up tomorrow at noon." He gave me a quick kiss on the top of the head. "Tell Ryann I said hi."

Stunned, I turned and staggered toward Ryann's porch. At her door, I looked back and watched Asher walk around the front of his truck, open the door, and slide in behind the wheel. He started the engine and rolled down the passenger side window.

"Sleep tight, city girl." Then he pressed his lips to his fingertips and held them out to me before driving away.

Holy crap. What just happened?

CHAPTER TWENTY-FIVE
FREE NOW

"I still can't believe you're involved with Asher."

Ryann and I sat in her kitchen, tall glasses of sweet tea in front of us on the old farmhouse table. She'd greeted me at the door, relieved, she said, to see me since no one had heard from me in a while. She'd been doing homework at the house because Lad had a Light Council meeting and she took the opportunity to visit her parents. She was planning to head to Altum for the night soon.

"I can't believe it either," I said, tracing a pattern in the beads of condensation on the outside of the glass. What I really couldn't believe was that my glamour hadn't worked on him. What did it mean? "It all kind of... happened. I can't really explain it."

She smiled and took a sip from her tea. "Some things are just meant to be—you can't fight them. Lad and I tried. I broke up with him once because I thought I was doing the best thing for him. He did the same thing, sending me away because he was trying to protect me. But in the end, nothing could stop us from being together. If it's meant to happen, it will."

I shook my head. "It *shouldn't* happen with Asher."

"Why? Because he's human?"

"That and… he's too nice for me. He's a good guy. I mean a *really* good guy."

Her expression quirked in confusion. "And you can't be with a good guy?"

Shaking my head again, I swallowed a lump in my throat. "You know what I did to Lad—and to you. I almost ruined your relationship. I've done things equally as bad—worse maybe."

"Yes. And we *forgave* you because you were sorry and you did your best to make things right. Just because you've done bad things doesn't mean you're permanently damaged and condemned to be alone forever—or to be with some guy who treats you badly or something. You've *changed*, Ava. You want to do the right thing and make better choices. You deserve a second chance. You deserve good things in life. But me telling you that isn't going to make a difference, is it? I said it on the day of your wreck, and I'll say it again. You have to forgive *yourself* before you'll be able to move on from your past and accept the happiness that's waiting for you in your future."

For some reason, Ryann's words caused my eyes to fill up and my mouth to tremble. I drowned the uncomfortable reaction in a big swallow of sweet tea.

"What was it like… to find out… everything, after growing up in the human world?"

Ryann gave me a knowing smile. "It was a shock, but Asher can take it. I've known him since I was in kindergarten. He's about the most accepting person I've ever met. He's never seemed to see skin color or social class at all when it comes to choosing friends. And he's got the calmest, steadiest outlook on life. When we were in the tenth grade, a meteorite hit out near Coffeeville. There were all kinds of rumors about aliens—you know how people are. Some people were scared, but Asher was the first one out on the site, ready to introduce himself to our extra-planetary visitors. Believe me, if *anyone* can handle this, it's him."

I nodded, hearing it all but afraid to believe it.

Seeing that I wasn't going to respond, Ryann pushed back from the table. "I think we should go tell Lad what you've learned about Audun's plans. His council meeting should be over by now. Ready to go to Altum?"

* * *

When I'd left this place a week ago, I'd never expected to return. Now I was standing in the heart of Altum, looking at the most fantastic production operation I could possibly have imagined.

"We're back in business." Ryann smiled and gestured to the roomful of Elven people working behind her.

I was sure it was quite different from what the factory in town had looked like. Huge copper pots stood over fires, steam rising from their open tops. Further down the line, Elves worked together using a pulley system and large funnels to pour the freshly brewed tea into glass bottles. Others affixed caps and labels and loaded the bottles into crates.

"Pretty soon we'll be up to the level of production where we were before the explosion. And there's plenty of room here to expand if we want to. The location is secure, the people of the Light Court understand how important it is and are willing to pitch in, and now we don't even have to transport the saol water off-site. We just have to bring the tea bags and bottles here. Other than the job loss in Deep River, this is actually better."

"How many humans were left unemployed?" I asked. One more thing to feel guilty about.

"Around two hundred. But I've signed a contract with a distributor to take the tea worldwide, and I'll be able to employ some of them in my business office and advertising department and as delivery drivers. I'm using the insurance money to help the rest retrain and look for new jobs."

"That's great." I looked past her toward a figure approaching in the distance. "Lad's coming."

Though I'd been welcomed to attend their wedding and invited to stay in Altum, though Ryann stressed I'd been *forgiven*, I still felt weird about seeing him again. The memory of what I'd done to him was still too fresh in my mind. Probably because I'd repeated my crimes in Nashville and New York. Had I really changed? Did I really deserve another chance? It didn't feel like it.

When Lad reached us, he wrapped his arms around Ryann and kissed her then turned to me with an outstretched hand. "Ava—welcome back. I'm glad you reconsidered and decided to stay with us."

"Oh—no. I'm not. I mean, I'm only here long enough to fill you in on what I learned about S and what Audun's planning to do with it."

"I see." He frowned. "Where's Culley?"

Lad's tone was dark, and I knew why. He was infuriated with Culley for what he'd done to Ryann—he'd sworn to make him pay for it someday. Maybe he thought I wouldn't stay because Culley and I were together for real now.

"Back in New York. I... left him." He'd given me no choice with his abrupt confession—not to mention the way he'd pushed me at Asher. "Apparently, he was in on it from the start. He told me. He took something from the saol water distillery here—it's in the drug Audun plans to use to enslave and destroy the humans."

Lad and Ryann looked at each other, clearly dismayed.

"Remember the saol—the drink you tasted during the wedding ceremony?" he asked her.

She nodded. "Yes, one sip just about laid me out for the night."

"It's highly intoxicating and extremely habit-forming. Even more so when it's boiled down to crystal form—our people used to administer it for pain relief in case of traumatic accidents or in ancient times to help those injured in battle. But we stopped using it because a mere speck of it is enough to produce intoxication and addiction. That must be what he took—that's what he was doing in the saol water room the night we fought. He wasn't following me. I just happened to be there when he was trying to sneak away with his contraband." He groaned. "We *showed* him the saol-making process. He could help the Dark Elves replicate it for themselves."

I nodded sadly. "I had begun to think there was some hope for Culley. He intervened for me with his father—he protected me. I think there's good in him, but he's trying so hard to please Audun he's blinded to the harm he's causing."

"Well, we can't worry about him right now," Lad said. "We have to start working on a solution to this problem. This substance is too strong even for Elves—humans can't handle it. They'll keep using it until it kills them. We have to do something to stop the spread of the drug."

"Maybe Nox can intervene?" I suggested. He was the Dark King, and though the Dark Council wasn't loyal to him, many of his subjects were.

Lad shook his head. "I'll speak to him immediately, but he's in Japan right now. He took Vancia abroad again because of the threat of assassination—and he's been making connections with the global tribes, ensuring their support. Hopefully together, they'll be able to stand against Audun's coup attempt."

"*If* he can trust them," I said. "Be sure he knows Falene, the ruler over Australia, is loyal to Audun. She's his wife. And Culley's mother. From what I hear, she's very strong."

"I will," he said. "Let's go to the palace and discuss what you've learned."

I gave him all the information I had—the information from the news, and what Audun had said himself when he'd unashamedly claimed responsibility for the epidemic.

"He intends to take over not only the Dark Court but the world. I guess he thinks when he's decimated the human population, the other Elves will either be so grateful they'll give him their loyalty—or so afraid of him they won't stand in his way," I said. "I know how his mind works. Believe me—he'll stop at nothing."

"What I can't believe is how bold he is, when he's not even the rightful heir to the throne," Lad said. "And you're sure Culley is loyal to him?"

"I don't know what else to think—Culley sent me away. He refused to come with me. He said he had to stay with his father. And he was out at nightclubs every night while we were in the city. I thought at first he was just keeping up his old habits, or that he was avoiding me for some reason. Now I think he was probably pushing the S." The thought made me sadder than I could express. There was so much potential in Culley, but apparently his father's influence was too strong.

"Well thank you for bringing us this information and putting yourself at risk to get it. I'm thankful you're safe. I'm sure you want to rest from your journey now. What will you do next?"

"Whatever she wants, right Ava?" Ryann said. "You're free now. Your life is your own to do anything you want with it."

I nodded, smiling weakly. It was a nice sentiment but it wasn't true. I couldn't do *anything* I wanted. What I wanted was to stay in Deep River—to stay with Asher.

Obviously reading my emotions, Ryann patted my back. "You don't have to leave him you know." She glanced over at Lad, and from the way his brows lifted and the way his surprised gaze shifted to me, she must have told him about my attachment to the human guy.

"Have you told him the truth?" he asked.

"Asher? You mean about... us? No, of course not. I know the rules."

Lad grinned. "The rules aren't all they're cracked up to be—not all of them anyway. Did you know Ryann's grandmother fell in love with a human? She married him—left it all behind."

I blinked several times, surprised. "No, well, yes I guess I knew there was a human there somewhere in the family tree. I never heard the story though."

"There's not that much to it," she explained. "She met him in these woods and said that was it for her—she knew she had to be with him no matter what. She never told him the secret, and he never demanded to know about her past. They made it work—I wouldn't be here if they hadn't. She lost him young, but she says she has no regrets. Their love was worth it."

Lad stepped close to Ryann and wrapped an arm around her waist, pulling her in tightly to his side. "I felt the same way. I would have walked away from my kingdom and never looked back, if that's what it took. It wouldn't have been easy, but I'd have done anything it took to be with her—because I love her." He paused. "Do you love him, Ava?"

"Oh—I…" My face flamed, and my heart exploded in a frenzy of erratic beats. Which made me suspicious. *Did* I love him? I hadn't allowed myself to go there. Every time I started thinking along those lines, I had shut down that path of thought and veered off in another direction. Because there was no point in it.

Asher was certainly deserving of love. In spite of his fear he wasn't hero material, he'd come through for me over and over again. He was smart, and capable, and sweet, and funny, and loyal—and so good-looking I lost my breath just thinking about it. I'd never felt like this about anyone ever. When I thought about leaving town and never seeing him again, a jagged pain ripped through my chest.

I did love him.

Oh wow. And *oh no.* What was I supposed to do with *that*? I wasn't even sure about the extent of his feelings for me—I thought they were pretty serious, but he hadn't said the words.

Even if he *did* love me, too, my being with him could put him in danger. Suppose Audun wanted to hunt me down and bring me back? Culley had seen Asher. He knew he lived somewhere in Deep River. Asher said his farm was outside the town limits, but it couldn't be too far out there. As clever and alluring as Culley was, it would take him about two minutes with one of Asher's female classmates to get the location of his home. Could I protect Asher somehow? I'd never tried my glamour on Culley. But it was *possible*…

"You have to at least try, Ava. Tell him the truth," Ryann urged. "Give him the choice. If he can't handle it, you can always remove the memory."

"I'm not sure that's true. I did try… earlier tonight. To make him forget me." I took a shuddering breath, remembering the experience. "It didn't seem to work."

Lad and Ryann exchanged astounded expressions. "That's… strange," Lad said. "It certainly worked on me. Have you ever had that happen before?"

"No. Well, I mean I've encountered people who seemed more resistant than others but it's never failed completely. I'm not sure what went wrong."

Ryann studied me thoughtfully for a few seconds. "Maybe you didn't *want* it to work."

"What? No. I *was* trying. I wanted to do what was best for him, and forgetting me is definitely in his best interests."

"Well, I know I have to want to read someone's emotions or to exert my Sway," she said. "I have to mean it, to want to. And Lad's leadership glamour didn't present itself until he'd accepted he *would* be the Light King and actually wanted the job."

"That's true," Lad said.

"Maybe a part of you didn't want Asher to be able to forget you," Ryann suggested.

"I don't know." But maybe she was right. The idea of erasing all the precious time we'd spent together had nearly killed me. I'd forced myself to say the words, but my heart hadn't been in the act.

Though I'd used my glamour on him, Asher remembered everything. And I was *glad* he did. For the first time in a long time, there was a flicker of lightness in my chest. A funny feeling, it was something like… hope. Maybe there *was* a way to be with him. Maybe, like Ryann's human grandfather, he'd accept that I could never tell him the full truth of my past. Maybe he'd be satisfied with part of me, since I couldn't offer him all of me. It was worth a try.

Ryann's sympathetic expression morphed into a smile. "What are you thinking?"

I smiled back at her. "I was wondering… is there any chance you have something I could borrow that would be appropriate for a Pecan Picking Party?"

Chapter Twenty-Six
Family

True to his word, Asher pulled up to Ryann's house right at noon the next day. Big Red was spotless and shining. Asher didn't look so bad himself.

Wearing a crisp pinstriped blue button down and a pair of jeans with his ever-present boots, he looked ready to film a manly cologne commercial or praise the virtues of Chevy or Dodge in a way that would have men *and* women rushing to the dealerships to buy. His smile was brilliant and tinged with male appreciation as he gave me an appraising once-over.

"Well look at you. Looks like you had a *full* night of beauty sleep and then some."

He met me at the bottom of the porch steps and kissed my heated cheek then waved to Ryann's mom who was visible in the kitchen window. Taking my hand, he led me to his truck and opened the door for me.

I fidgeted in my seat, breathing shallowly, as he walked around and got in his side. I'd rarely felt so nervous in my life. This was a big day. Asher started the truck and smiled over at me. "*Did* you sleep? Or did you two girls stay up and talk all night?"

I let out a nervous laugh. "We did talk a lot. And no… I didn't really sleep that great," I admitted.

"Me either." He winked as he put the truck in gear. "I was missing my sleeping bag buddy."

My face heated and grew several shades darker. Asher didn't have sexual glamour, but he certainly had *something* that was working for me.

He wasn't kidding when he said the farm was outside the town limits. We drove at least twenty minutes before turning down a gravel road marked by a huge dairy barn. Another mile or two until the farmhouse came into view. And by farmhouse, I mean a beautiful old home, painted white with a wraparound porch, set back from the road with a long tree-lined driveway leading up to it. Its windows sparkled in the midday sun like jewels. At the end of the drive stood a mailbox emblazoned with the name McCord.

"The family farm, huh?"

He shrugged, wearing a cheeky grin. "It's a farm. And my family lives here. Don't be *too* impressed. We have a lot of land, but we're not rich by any stretch. Granddaddy bought the land a long time ago when it was literally dirt cheap. A place like this requires a lot of upkeep… and a lot of work—most of which is done by Granddaddy and me."

We didn't turn into the driveway, but passed it by, driving past a cornfield, several fields of row crops, and an orchard before he took a right onto a narrow gravel road.

"Are the pecan trees back here?"

Asher smiled. "No. Those giant trees you saw running up and down the length of the drive? Those are the pecan trees. There's a grove back behind the house, too."

"So what are we doing back here then?"

"*We* are going in the back gate. Don't worry. We'll still end up at the house. Granddaddy suggested it—he thought you might like to see the property."

"Oh yes. That would be great."

I sat up straighter in my seat and took in the view as we continued down the small lane that apparently bordered the McCord homestead. There were two ponds, lots and lots of rolling pastures and trees, and more cows than I could count.

I glanced over at him. "You're a cowboy," I said in amusement.

He slid a flirty glance in my direction. "That depends— do you like cowboys?"

I nodded. "I think I do."

His smile widened. "Then, yes ma'am, I am."

Reaching the end of the gravel lane, Asher stopped the truck. Right in front of us was a large metal gate connected to the barbed wire fence enclosing the entire property.

"Be right back," he said and slid out of the truck, pulling a key from his pocket and unlocking the padlock that held its chain closure in place.

He pushed the heavy iron gate open and gestured for me to get behind the wheel and pull the truck forward. Feeling a little nervous to drive the huge machine, I did as he asked. Then he re-chained and locked the gate and got back into the truck.

"That seems very secure," I commented.

"It keeps the cows in," he said blandly. "Granddaddy has his way of doing things, and I don't argue. I'm not sure if I've mentioned it, but he's a bit eccentric."

I smiled. "How eccentric?"

He laughed. "Well, for instance, when he bought this piece of land, he had a trench dug around the entire thing and had a cast iron pipe laid all the way around it."

"A pipe? For irrigation?"

"Nope. He says it's to protect against earthquakes. The New Madrid fault line is only sixty miles from here you know."

"Oookay." I laughed.

"Yep. And… well, you'll see. He's pretty superstitious, but he's a great guy."

"I know he is—he raised you, didn't he?"

"He did that," Asher agreed. "For better or worse."

The innocent phrase got my nerves going all over again, thinking about the confessions I'd have to make if I were going to stay with Asher. Would he want *me*—for better or worse? That was, would he still want me with him once I told him the truth about myself and my family?

I hoped so. I couldn't stay with him and continue to deceive him, especially if it might put him in danger.

Someday someone might come looking for me, and he had to know what he might be dealing with. At the very least he'd understand if I suddenly disappeared someday and not think I'd abandoned him like his no-good father had. If I made the decision to commit to this, I'd never leave him voluntarily, but someone might come and take me against my will.

Asher reached across the seat and took my hand, and I squeezed his fingers tightly, schooling my face into a pleasant expression, though my heart and mind were all over the place. I wasn't sure what to do. I wanted to be with him. But I might not be good for him.

And after I told him the truth, he might not want me anymore anyway. In spite of how "calm" and "accepting" Ryann said he was, there was a good chance Asher would not even believe me. No matter what happened, at least we had today. Come tonight, I'd need to decide one way or the other, but I didn't want to think about that now.

The truck crested a hill, giving us a beautiful view of the house and fields below. Several cars were parked in the circular drive in front of the house now, and another was making its way up the long drive.

Asher put the truck in park but left it running. He shifted to face me. "I've always loved this spot. I used to think it would be the perfect place to build a house someday. Well, until I decided I wanted to leave this place. Now I'm thinking… well, I can see that old vision again." He drew a picture in the air with his fingers. "The front door facing this way, overlooking the valley, a swing set and a pool in the back, a garden plot right over there." He turned back to me. "I think I just needed to meet the right person to appreciate that old dream—someone who made me want to stay and helped me see the value of what I already have."

Taking in what I thought was the meaning of his words, I swallowed hard, my heart racing. It was the perfect opening to speak up and be honest with him, to tell him I wanted all that, too. To tell him the truth. But I couldn't speak. I was still too afraid. And the timing was terrible. The party was about to begin.

When I didn't respond, Asher nodded. "Okay then. We should go. Everybody will be waiting for us. Just think about what I said."

He shifted the truck into drive again and eased it down the hill toward the house, parking it in front of a three-car garage.

We hadn't even made it to the house before I saw his grandfather approaching with a wide smile and a slight limp—it had to be him. The love and pride on his face as he looked at Asher erased any other possibility.

"So *this* is the city lass we've heard so much about," he called out. Contrary to what I'd pictured, Asher's granddaddy was not an old southern gentleman. His voice was not tinged with the slow and sweet Deep South accent. He sounded like he was right off a plane from Scotland.

I flared my eyelids at Asher as I whispered, "You never said he was Scottish."

He grinned. "You never asked."

Mr. McCord reached us and took my hands, holding them out to the side and looking me over. "It's been a long time since I've seen a… California girl. Welcome darlin' to our humble home."

Asher laughed. "Are you flirting with my girl, Granddaddy?"

"Mebbe," he said in his soft brogue, a twinkle in his eye. "Mebbe so. I hear you had quite an adventure on the way here, but you're home now, and it's the safest place for you both. Well, come on then to the house. Your mother's got herself all worked up over meeting this young lady. Let's go show her off."

Together we went inside, stepping into a kitchen that was warm, fragrant, and bustling with people.

"Momma," Asher called.

A woman turned away from the huge pot she was stirring. Her eyes landed first on Asher then shifted quickly to me. First they widened then crinkled in the same way her son's always did when he smiled. She lay the spoon on a plate and moved toward us, holding out her arms.

"Oh my goodness. Ava. It's so wonderful to meet you. Asher has told me good things, and I can see why. You're even lovelier than he described."

"That's because she's beyond description," he said proudly.

I rolled my eyes. "Thank you both. It's so nice to meet you Ms. McCord. Your home is so pretty."

"Well thank you honey. At the moment it's chock full. I don't even know why I bothered to clean the whole house—every single person crams into the kitchen. And you just call me Jenna." Lifting her voice to be heard over all the chatter, she said, "Let's move outside everybody. It's picking time!"

Turning back to me, she asked, "How was your trip from New York? You do so much traveling for such a young person. And Asher told me you're going to be in a commercial!"

I answered her questions, and she chattered happily as we moved out to the back lawn where wooden picnic tables were set up under a grove of pecan trees. Atop the tables were aluminum tubs filled with ice and assorted beverages. Large buckets lined the patio, ready to be filled with a sweet, nutty harvest.

Granddaddy spoke up, getting the event started. "Most of you have been with us many times before. For those of you who are new pickers..." He swung a glance over at me and winked. "...it's pretty simple. Fill your bucket and come back for another if you like. You keep what you pick up, try not to give yourself a bellyache along the way from eating nuts as you go, and save some room for chili and cornbread afterward. Let the picking begin!"

The party guests grabbed buckets and got to work, moving through the grove and scooping fallen pecans from the ground. A few decided to forego the crowded back yard and headed around the house toward the front. That was Asher's strategy.

He grabbed my hand and two buckets. "Come on. I think the ones from the front yard taste better."

We strolled among the trees as a warm breeze blew the leaves over our heads. After dropping a few handfuls of pecans into my bucket I decided to crack one and taste it.

"I've never had a pecan that didn't come from the grocery store already shelled."

Asher gave me a mock-offended glare. "Then you haven't lived. We've got to fix that immediately."

I stepped on one of the nuts, cracking the shell under my shoe then picked it up to extract what was left of the crushed pecan inside. It was a challenge. Tiny bits of shell were imbedded into the nut meat.

Asher brushed it from my hand. "*What* are you doing? You mangled that poor pecan. Watch and learn, padawan."

He placed two pecans in his palm, closed his fingers, and squeezed. A cracking noise emanated from inside his fist. When he opened it, both pecan shells were open. "Ta da." He smiled.

I plucked one of them from his hand and pulled a perfectly intact pecan half from the shell, popping it into my mouth. I couldn't believe how plump and juicy it was. I smiled at Asher.

"You are so right about these *front yard* pecans. Let's get them all before anybody else figures it out."

He laughed, and we ran around, gathering as many as we could as fast as we could. When our buckets were both overflowing, he took my hand and led me to a tree swing suspended from one of the thick, high branches.

"Here, I'll push you." He pulled the swing seat back. "You deserve a break after your Olympic pecan picking performance."

I gave him a sassy side glance and sat in the swing. "Beginner's luck."

Asher pulled the ropes back and let them go, sending me gliding forward. My belly did a pleasant swoop I hadn't felt since swinging as a child.

"No, you're a natural," he said. "You're a *born* pecan picker."

I glanced back over my shoulder at him. "This is a really fun day."

"Oh, you haven't even *seen* fun yet." His tone held a teasing warning. When the momentum carried me back toward him, he placed his hands on my upper hips and gave a firm push, sending the swing rocketing forward again.

I squealed as I sailed up, up toward the blue sky and green leaves and fell back again to feel Asher's big hands around my waist once more, propelling me for another skyward ride.

The experience brought back joyful memories of swinging in my backyard in California with my dad as he pushed me and dared me to go higher and higher, to conquer my fear of falling and embrace the freedom of being slightly out of control. When I thought about it, that's how I always felt with Asher, out of control, yet also safe, somehow.

The day ended with a casual outdoor dinner of steaming chili and honey-buttered cornbread and naturally, pecan pie. The conversation around the picnic tables was loud and good-natured. I met Asher's extensive network of aunts and uncles and cousins and family friends.

Overall, they were a remarkable family—not because of what they'd accomplished or what they owned, but because of the way they loved and accepted each other. It was a whole new thing in my experience.

After the last of the guests had driven away with their pecan hauls, Asher walked me out to the carriage house where my guest room was located. It was a separate building from the main house, but no less inviting. Sided in white clapboard, it had three old fashioned looking garage doors across the front with a dormered window above each one. The windows were flanked by black shutters, and each had a window box planter filled with fall blooms. To one side was a red brick chimney, and near it, a ground floor entrance to the apartment above the garage.

The sun had set, and the sounds of singing frogs and whirring cicadas filled the night air. At the door, Asher stopped and turned me to face him, stroking underneath my chin with the side of his finger. "I'm not gonna come up because if I do, I won't want to leave. And there's no way my mom will miss it if I don't happen to be in my bed tonight—makes me wish I'd already moved into this place."

Blushing at his obvious reference to his desire for me, I avoided the subject entirely. "This is going to be yours?"

"Yeah—the plan was I'd move out here until I got ready to build my own house up on that hill I showed you. It's an apartment with a full kitchen, a nice bathroom, fireplace and all. I guess I was putting off moving my stuff over here because it would have seemed like some kind of commitment to stay on the farm. Until I met you, I wasn't ready to do that."

"But now you want to?"

He nodded and leaned in for a soft kiss. "I do. If you're gonna be here, too." He hesitated, staring directly into my eyes. His held some clouds, something unsettled.

"Ava—I think you probably guessed this already since I drove all over Kingdom Come to go get you and bring you back here, but I care about you. A lot. I want you to know that. Now I know you've had some trouble in your past, and you don't like to talk about it. But over there in that house are the two *other* people I care about most in this world. And I have to make sure I do right by them. They love you." He hesitated a minute. "*I* love you…"

"You do?"

"Yes. I do. I'm completely, totally, one hundred percent in love with you. Now will you let me finish?"

"Um, yes. Okay." His shocking statement had my mind spinning so fast I wasn't sure I'd be able to comprehend anything else he had to say.

"You fit right in here, and I can easily see bringing you into our family and keeping you here forever, but… you've got a lot of secrets."

That's when my heart seized up and stopped beating. Of course he was worried about my evasiveness and mysterious past—he'd be a fool not to be concerned. He wanted answers, and I couldn't blame him. My hopes of hiding my shameful past from him were dashed. But how could I tell him the truth? Heart thrashing inside my chest, I stayed quiet as he continued.

"After what you said to me last night outside Ryann's house, the way you seemed to be almost ordering me to forget you like some kind of hypnotist or something, I think there might be more to your secrets than I realized."

I broke free from his arms and started for the driveway, overcome by panic. "I'll go. I'm sorry. I'm so sorry—for everything."

Asher's hand caught my shoulder and stopped me. He stepped in front of me, blocking my retreat. "Whoa there. I tell you I'm in love with you and you're ready to bolt? I don't think so. You're stuck with me now, city girl. What I'm saying is—I've never felt this way about anybody. I didn't even know it was possible. And I want you—no matter *what* the truth of the situation is. But I do need the truth. I'm ready to commit to this thing for the long haul. But I need the same from you. I need you to let me know you for real—all of you. I need you to trust me enough to be honest with me, or this is not going to work out. Do you think you can do that?"

I stared at him a long moment before dropping my gaze to the paver stones and his big boots bracketing my feet between them. "I don't know," I whispered. "I'm scared."

"'Course you are," he said. "It's scary to make yourself vulnerable to somebody. Don't you think I was scared to tell you I love you? I've been screaming it inside my head for the past three days, but I didn't know if I'd ever get up the guts to say it."

"This is different," I said. "What I have to say would change everything. It will make you see me differently. You might even change your mind about how you feel."

His fingers gripped my upper arms. "*Nothing* will change the way I feel about you—that's a promise."

I shook my head. "You don't know that."

I was so torn. I knew exactly where he was coming from. He was saying basically the same things to me that I'd said to Culley. How could a relationship have any chance of survival without honesty? But how could I be honest about myself, about my past—my very existence for God's sake—without causing Asher to hate me or freak out and run the other way?

"Can I... can I have some time to think about it?" I asked.

"Of course." Asher wrapped an arm around my shoulders and walked me back to the carriage house door. "And while you're thinking about it, remember this."

He dipped his head and kissed me, so sweetly, so deeply, with so much passion I nearly forgot the past myself.

"All right, city girl. You get some sleep. In the morning, we'll see about getting you that rental car and maybe put you to work—show you what being a farm girl is like."

I nodded. "That sounds good."

Then I opened the door and climbed the stairs to the apartment, where I'd either spend the night... or pack up my things and leave this little piece of paradise, once and for all.

CHAPTER TWENTY-SEVEN
TWO OF A KIND

I couldn't say how many times during the night I changed my mind.

I tossed and turned in the large bed, despite its comfort. On one hand, there was the Elven obligation to keep the secret. On the other, Asher. On one hand, I'd be risking a lot by telling him the truth—he could laugh at me and think I was crazy, or he could *believe* me and be afraid of me or disgusted by the things I'd done instead of loving me. On the other hand—Asher—and his very legitimate desire to actually know the person he was committing his life to.

When the sun rose in the morning, I was still awake. And I was still there.

I would tell him. I would tell him everything—who I was, what I'd done, what Audun and Culley had done, and what they planned to do, about the danger to the human population. I would put all my cards on the table and see if

Asher could handle the ones he'd been given. I loved him. He said he loved me. He deserved a chance to prove it.

I got up and showered, dressed, and nervously made my way down the stairs to go to the main house. When I opened the carriage house door, I heard shouting.

It was my name. Someone was shouting my name. "Ava!"

It was a male voice, and assuming it was Asher's, I broke into a run, calling his name in response.

And then I heard the voice in my head.

Ava, it's me.

My feet stopped dead in their tracks. My eyes scanned the surroundings searching for him. There at the end of the driveway was Culley's rented Jaguar.

He wasn't in the car but standing in the street, pitched forward with his hands on his knees as if he'd run a marathon and was fighting for breath at the finish line. My heart clenched into a tight ball. He'd found me. He'd found Asher's house.

Just as I'd always feared, I'd brought danger to Asher, and now to his family as well. Had Audun sent Culley to kill me or just to bring me back? And why had Culley stopped there? Why hadn't he driven up to the house and boldly announced himself as I would have expected him to?

What are you doing here? I asked him.

I need to talk to you.

Right.

Honestly. I only want to talk. No one knows I'm here. No one even knows about your little human pet, so you don't have to worry about him. This is about me and you. I couldn't let things end the way they did in New York—not without telling you everything.

It's a little late for that.

Please, Ava. I drove all night. He straightened to standing but then staggered to the side and nearly fell over, looking drunk.

What is the matter with you? I asked, taking a step in his direction down the drive.

I don't know. I feel sick.

Was he faking? Was it a trick to get me away from the house? I stopped and glanced over at the front door, the windows with yellow light glowing inside. I didn't want Asher's mom or Grandpa to see Culley and worry. I didn't want anyone getting caught in the crossfire of whatever was going on between us—especially if Culley was here on Audun's behalf.

Jogging down the drive toward the street, I prayed Asher had slept in and didn't happen to open his window to take in the morning view. As I reached Culley's car I noticed the engine was still running, the door standing ajar. He still stood in the street. I didn't go out to him but stayed inside the low white rail fence bordering the front yard.

"What's the matter with your car?"

He shook his head, looking pasty and sweating at the temples. "Nothing. It's… it's me. I pulled in and felt like I couldn't drive another inch. I had to get out and chuck up."

"Oh. Well… I guess you shouldn't have driven all night. You're exhausted. It's not safe."

Culley gave a weak laugh. "Self-preservation isn't my number one concern these days."

It was strange to see him again, when I'd been so sure I never would. Though as handsome as ever, Culley seemed... diminished somehow. And it wasn't just his sickly state. His eyes looked hollow, the skin of his face stretched unnaturally tight. The anger I held toward him crumbled a bit around the edges.

Folding my arms over my chest, I took a step closer to him. "So... you said you wanted to talk. About what?"

He took a breath and stood straighter. "I wanted to tell you..." Culley paused and took a few more breaths. "... to tell you I'm sorry. For stealing the saol from Altum. For the S situation. You asked me before if I knew what my father would do with it. I didn't know, and I didn't care. But I should have cared. I do now, and I regret what I've done."

"Okay... and you drove all night to tell me this *why?*"

"I want you to forgive me. I couldn't stand the way you looked at me there at the parade when I told you about my part in the spread of S. I haven't been able to sleep or eat since you left. I want... I want you to come with me. I can change. I *have* changed. I can be a decent bond-mate—if you'll give me a chance. We can go anywhere you want—take that trip to Savannah, go back to that hotel you love in Nashville—anywhere."

The desperate offer and vulnerable expression he wore caused my heart to tug in his direction. "Culley..."

This was terrible. I hated seeing him like this. He was so distraught—so broken. I took another step toward the fence.

The sound of shoes slapping against the driveway caused me to spin around toward the house. Asher was running down the drive, a fierce expression on his face. His grandfather walked behind him, carrying a rifle.

Oh my God. I turned back to Culley. "Just leave, okay?"

His expression was resolute. "Not without you."

Culley please. You shouldn't even want me. You and I… we're not in love.

It doesn't matter, Angel. I want you anyway. We're two of a kind. We're good together. That's as good as it gets in this life.

You're wrong. You're only saying that because you've never been in love. I have. I took a deep breath and released it. *I love him, Culley.*

Culley stood up straight and swayed back, looking like he'd been slapped. But then he set his jaw in determination, keeping his gaze steadily fixed on mine even as Asher approached.

When Asher reached me, he pulled me to him, wrapping a protective arm around my shoulders. His rapid breaths were audible. "You okay?" he asked between them.

I nodded, and he turned his attention to Culley. "What can we do for you… *mate*?" He bit off the last word, making it sound exactly like the challenge it was.

Culley's hands curled into fists. He lifted his chin and stood a little taller, though he still looked queasy. "*You* can go back up to the house and let Ava and me finish our conversation. We'll both be out of your hair soon enough and you can go back to reading the Farmer's Almanac, or whatever the hell it is you people do around here."

The muscles in Asher's neck went rigid. "She's not going *anywhere* with you. This is her home now."

"It's true," I said to Culley. "I've made a decision. This is where I want to be." Silently I added, *I'm staying with Asher. Please try to understand.*

I could see in his eyes he believed me now. They closed in a long, slow blink before he opened them again and gave me a pleading glance. *You're the one who doesn't understand. If you won't have me... I'm afraid of what's going to become of me. I need you, Ava.*

My heart tore, one part pulling toward the guy at my side the other toward the guy pouring his out in the street. But it wasn't right—for either of us.

No, Culley. You need someone you can really open up to. You'll never be happy until you let your guard down and open your heart and let someone see the real you.

That's the thing, isn't it? He huffed a humorless laugh though his face was contorted in misery. *No one can see the real me—except for you. You've asked me what I really look like. Well, you're looking at him. You're the only person I've ever met who looks at me and sees the same thing I see in the mirror. You see* me. *But it doesn't seem to matter. You don't want the real me.*

Again my heart squeezed, but I stood my ground. He didn't need my sympathy—he needed a real, eternal connection with someone he truly loved. That wasn't me.

And he was right—he *wasn't* the one I loved, the one I needed.

Someone will, Culley. I promise you, someone will.

He barked out a sharp, bleak laugh and turned around, stalking away, as if he meant to hike out to the highway on foot and leave his expensive car idling in front of us.

Granddaddy spoke up. "Asher, son, why don't you go ahead and pull that young man's car back out onto the street for him? Looks like he could use a hand."

"Yeah, a hand… or my boot in his ass," Asher muttered. But he followed his grandfather's instructions, backing the car onto the county road then getting out of it and calling to Culley. "Hey—here you go. Now why don't you get inside and get the hell out of here? And don't bother coming back. Ava's happy with me, and I plan to keep it that way."

Culley did an about face and stalked back toward Asher, his face stiff with fury, his eyes flashing icy fire.

"You don't even *know* her mate. She's not who you think she is. She's not like you, not like the old man there, not like anyone you've ever met. She's like me—we *belong* together. Has she told you the truth about herself? No, I can see from your face she hasn't. Ever wondered why? Because you're not enough for her, man. You never will be. She's too good for you, too good for any human, and when she's done slumming she'll leave you and come back to me. I'll be waiting, and I promise you—I can wait longer than you can."

Asher shook his head. I wasn't sure if it was in sympathy or disgust. "You smug asshole. You better get in this fancy car and get the hell out of here right now. And if I were you, I wouldn't drive through town—they're looking for somebody who fits your description for the tea plant bombing."

Culley laughed bitterly. "Oh that's rich—my description. You know, while you're pointing fingers, farm boy, you might as well turn one to your girlfriend there. We were in on it together, you know. That's the kind of thing we do, and the factory's not the worst of it. But don't take my word for it—ask her."

My mouth fell open at his mean-spirited lie about me. Was he also lying about himself? He'd told me mind to mind he hadn't been involved in the explosion, but now I didn't know what to believe.

With a wink, he shot me a silent parting remark. *Good luck Angel.* Then he reached into his pocket, pulled something out of it, and tossed it on the road. My wallet. Culley had it all along. He must have taken it from the crash site the day of the explosion, ensuring I'd need him and be forced to go with him. Sliding in behind the wheel, he peeled away, spinning his wheels in the gravel and kicking up a cloud of gray dust in his wake.

Asher turned to face me, still standing in the road. "Ava?" His voice was as troubled as his expression.

"No, Asher, he's lying." I started toward him, but his grandfather put a hand on my arm to stop me.

"I don't think you want to walk through that gate, young lady. Just wait for him to come to you."

Breaking away from Mr. McCord, I ran toward Asher. When I reached the end of the driveway, a wave of pain slammed into me, knocking me to my knees as if I'd run into a solid wall.

Asher was at my side in seconds. "Ava, what's wrong? What happened?"

I shook my head, feeling disoriented and nauseous. "I... don't know. I don't feel good."

Granddaddy's shoes came into view. He leaned down and slipped a hand under my arm. "Come on, son, let's get her up to the house. She'll be all right in a little while." He sounded entirely unworried.

"*What* is going on?" Asher asked. "What's wrong with her? Why do I feel like everyone knows something I don't?"

The two of them helped me to my feet and supported me as we made our way up the drive. I couldn't speak, fighting down wave after wave of nausea and focusing on putting one foot in front of the other.

"Tell you what," Granddaddy said. "Why don't you two go on up to the apartment and have a chat? I'll go fetch Miss Ava's coin purse from the road and then tell your momma you two will be late for breakfast."

By the time we made it to the carriage house, my head was starting to clear, and my belly didn't feel quite so fragile. I turned to see Mr. McCord's knowing expression.

"Thank you... for everything this morning," I said, meeting his keen eyes. "Now I think I know why you said this farm is the safest place for me."

He nodded and gave me a wink. "You're quite welcome, lass. I've always said… Deep River's heaven on earth. Except for all the cursed Fae folk."

Then he turned and walked toward the house, leaving me alone with Asher and his open jaw.

Chapter Twenty-Eight
Eternity

"You feeling better now?"

I nodded in response to Asher's gentle voice, sitting in a chair in the apartment's small living area. He'd offered me a glass of cold water, and I'd taken a few sips, wishing it was saol water instead. No doubt it would have been much more useful to counteract iron poisoning.

He sat in the chair opposite me, leaning forward, knees apart with his elbows resting on them and his hands clasped between them. His body bobbed back and forth in a tight rhythm as if the questions inside were about to burst out of him.

I couldn't blame him, but I still wasn't sure what I was going to say in response. Now that I was in the moment, saying these things out loud to him seemed incredibly stupid. He'd think I was nuts. And yet, I had no choice but to tell him the truth.

"I'm okay now. Thanks."

"Good." He stopped rocking. "What is going on here? What did Granddaddy mean? Why did you get sick?"

"Remember when you drove me onto your family's land through the back gate?"

"Yeah. Granddaddy said to bring you in that way so you could see the property."

"Right. I think he was also trying to prevent what just happened a few minutes ago. Somehow he knew. The pipe your grandfather laid all around the perimeter... it must have been made of pure iron—and I'm guessing the iron gate at the back spans the only break in the underground line. The pipe obviously runs under the front driveway."

"Okay... that still doesn't tell me what the hell is going on. What does all this have to do with you?"

My heart was fluttering so fast it felt like a moth desperately throwing itself against a pane of glass with a light inside. "The Fae folk he mentioned. I... I am one. Of them. Iron affects us. It makes us sick."

He sat back up with his hands braced on his knees, powerful arms locked tight, and a baffled expression on his face. "What does that mean? He told me stories when I was a kid but... I don't... are we talking like... fairies or something?" His tone showed his utter disbelief.

"It's... something like that. But different from what you might have read in the fairy tales. I don't even know where to begin. I thought about leaving last night so I could avoid this conversation, but then I decided early this morning to tell you everything. Now... I don't know how."

I started to rise from my chair. Asher's hand shot out and wrapped around my wrist. "Oh no. You're not going anywhere. I don't care where you start the story, just talk. Tell me, Ava. I love you. I just want the truth."

"You may not love me after you hear it."

"I told you last night—nothing will change the way I feel about you."

We'll see. "Okay, well... I guess I'll start with why I came here in the first place. I was on a mission from the Dark Court. They're... we are... I am... Elven. The center of the Light Court is here, just outside Deep River. I was visiting there as an emissary, but also as a spy."

He nodded slowly. "Those people I met the day of the crash, the ones you and Ryann were talking to. They're Fae... Elves, too?"

I was surprised how easily the E-word had rolled off his tongue. I was surprised he was still *talking* to me. How could he be so cool with it all? So far he was acting as if our being from two different species was no big deal.

"Yes. Lad and Vancia and Nox."

"I figured something was up—seeing you all together. And I knew there was something weird about that Nox guy, though I have to say, I never would have guessed *this*."

"You know you can't talk about this to *anyone*, right?"

"Of course. Although it seems like Granddaddy already knows something."

I glanced out the window overlooking the main house. "Yes. Seems like it. I'm not sure how that's possible, but I guess we'll find out soon enough."

He was quiet for a moment. "Culley said something about you being too good for a human guy. I guess that means... you're not human?"

I shook my head. "Not even a little bit."

"But you *look* human—actually no, check that—you look better than other people—all of you do. So... what else?"

I blinked. Blinked again. "What do you mean?"

"What else is different? I mean, other than being drop-dead gorgeous, what's the big deal?"

"Um... well, I'm immortal."

"Oh."

That one stunned him. He sat back in his chair and let out a long breath.

"And I have an unusually strong ability to influence people—it's called Sway."

"Is that what you were trying to do last night at Ryann's house? *Influence* me to forget you?"

I winced at the memory. "Sort of. Actually there's more to it. Each of us has at least one special ability—a glamour. Mine is memory manipulation."

All the things I'd told him up to that point hadn't seemed to faze him. But now—now his face hardened, and his brows lowered.

"So you were trying to use your special ability to make me forget all about you?"

"I tried. But it didn't work. I'm sorry. I thought it was the best thing for you. And also... I was afraid. I still am."

"Of me?"

"Of where this… this *thing* between us is going. . wanted to leave and make you forget me because there were all these things I couldn't tell you and all these big feelings, and I was worried about Culley showing up—which he did."

Asher's anger didn't seem to be dissipating. The volume of his voice ratcheted up—not shouting but clearly agitated. "Yes, he did, and it turned out fine. All the other stuff could have been solved by simply being open with me, trusting me a little bit. We're *all* afraid, Ava. I'm afraid of winding up a loser like my dad says. But I was willing to stay here— for you—to stay here *with* you. Forever. It's scary as hell to take that kind of risk for somebody, but you're worth it. I hoped you'd think I was worth it too. I thought you trusted me."

"I'm sorry," I repeated.

"Yeah well…" He got up and paced the room. He stopped. "What about now?"

"Now?"

"Do you trust me now?"

"I… well, yes, but…"

"But?"

"I still don't think you understand what you're getting into. And you still don't know everything I've done in service to Culley's father. I'm not sure I *want* you to know. I wish… I wish there *was* a future for us, but I'm not sure you're ready to live in my world—I don't know how you could be."

ing low on his hips, his head moved in a slow
walked to the door of the apartment. One
oorknob, he turned and looked back at me.

...problem isn't that I'm human and you're Elven…
or that I'm not 'ready' to live in your world. I think the
problem is *you're* not ready to forgive yourself for your past
and move on. You don't believe you deserve love. And
that—that's the one thing I can't help you with—that one
you've got to do for yourself."

Then he opened the door and left the apartment.

He left.

I knew it. I knew he couldn't handle it. It was too much
to expect. Slowly rising from my chair, I went to my packed
suitcase, taking the handle and lugging it down the stairs to
the apartment's outer door. The weight of the bag was
nothing compared to the weight in my chest.

It was over. The dream of being with him, of living in
this peaceful place and being part of his perfect family.
There was nothing left.

It was too bad my glamour *didn't* work on Asher. Not
so I could erase his memories of our conversation and my
revelation of the Elven secret. No, I would have used it to
make him forget my mistakes, to make him let me *stay.*

On second thought, no. I could never take advantage of
him and take away his choices. That wasn't love.

My wallet was at the bottom of the stairs where Mr.
McCord must have left it. Rolling my bag behind me down
the driveway, I headed for the county road that would take
me to the highway that would take me… where? To the

airport maybe? I had cash—I could buy a ticket, and now that I had my license back, I could fly. Somewhere.

Maybe I'd fly back to New York. Maybe Culley was right when he'd predicted I would come back to him. Why not? I couldn't be with the guy I loved, and I'd heard misery loved company. Culley and I could be miserable together.

No—I couldn't do that to him either. Even after what he'd done, there *was* still a chance for him if he could ever manage to be true to himself, defy his father, and make his own choices. There was bound to be someone out there who could manage to break through the Kevlar body armor he'd strapped around his heart. It just wasn't me.

Reaching the end of the driveway, I first threw my suitcase into the street. Then I prepared myself for the agony I knew was coming.

One… two… three…

I drew on all my strength and leapt from the end of the drive into the road. And immediately crumpled to the ground. The pain in my head was blinding. My arms and legs felt drained of energy. It was a good thing I hadn't had breakfast yet, because if I had, there would have been a mess on the road.

At least I knew what to do about it this time. Struggling to my hands and knees, I crawled forward, away from the iron-reinforced perimeter of the McCord property, dragging my rolling suitcase along beside me. The further away I got, the better I felt. After a few minutes I was able to get to my feet and then to walk. How far was it to the highway? I couldn't remember but it didn't really matter. I had all the time in the world and no idea what I was going to do with it.

Walking down the center of the narrow two-lane road, I listened to the birds, noting the colored leaves that would soon be falling, mentally saying good-bye to this place. I wouldn't be back. My business with the Light Court was concluded. It was possible Lad and Ryann would need further help from me, but we'd have to talk by phone. Even being in the same state with Asher would be torment if I couldn't be with him. I'd be too tempted to show up at his doorstep and beg him to take me back.

I shook my head and kicked a rock that had made its way onto the road. Asher was better off without me. That was the real reason I was leaving. I loved him, and I was letting him go.

It hit me then that maybe I *should* forgive myself—just a fraction. The fact I was willing to sacrifice my happiness for his had to count for something, right? I glanced back over my shoulder but the farmhouse was no longer visible.

Maybe someday after I'd done enough good to counter balance all the wrong I'd done... maybe then I *would* come back. And if Asher happened to still be here and happened to be unattached—

The sound of a vehicle approaching from behind made me move quickly to the left shoulder of the road. As brokenhearted as I was, I *did* want that shot at redemption—ending my life prematurely as roadkill would kind of put a damper on my comeback.

The color red filled my peripheral vision as th
pulled up beside me and slowed to a crawl. My heart wen.
from a steady thump-thump to whipping like a flag in a
tropical storm. I kept walking but glanced to the right when
the driver's window rolled down.

"Excuse me, miss? Do you have a problem?" Asher put
an elbow on the window frame and leaned out a bit. His
smile was huge and sent a surge of hope and love through
my heart.

Fighting for enough air to answer him, I said, "As a
matter of fact, I do. I've been a big jerk and blown my
chance with the guy I love."

"That does sound like a problem." He stopped the
truck, leaned over, and opened the passenger door. "Why
don't you climb in and we'll talk about it? I know a nice
place in town where they serve a killer breakfast. I don't
know about you, but I could go for some grits."

I stopped walking and stared at my dusty shoes. Then I
squeezed my eyelids closed, but it didn't help—the tears
leaked out anyway. Nodding, I walked around the front of
the truck and climbed up into the cab.

Asher put Big Red back into gear and resumed driving
toward the highway.

When I could finally manage it, I ventured a glance over
at his profile. He was still smiling.

"You know, I've been meaning to ask you this… what
on earth is a grit?"

His smile grew even larger and even sunnier. "I've been meaning to ask you something, too. What the heck does all this swirly foreign writing say?"

My jaw dropped as he extended his hand toward me and opened it. There in the center of his palm lay a familiar silver and gold braided band—with a notable addition. A beautiful diamond solitaire.

"It's the ring I gave you," I said, my voice choked with tears. I took it from him and studied it, turning it so the sun sparked in a prism pattern on the truck's interior.

"I had the diamond put on there before I headed to New York City to get you. But I left it here with Granddaddy for safekeeping." He winked. "Those big cities are full of shady characters, you know."

I let out a watery laugh, my joy competing with leftover tears. "They sure are."

"After we talked, I went to the house to get it from him—I wanted to show you that I love you and believe in you—no matter what you've done, no matter what comes," Asher said. "But Granddaddy was already out in the fields. I had to go searching for him to ask him where he'd put it. You know what he told me when I asked for it?"

I grinned, my vision blurred with happy tears. Shaking my head, I said, "No, but I can't wait to find out."

He said, "Son, it won't be easy, but the best apple is always on the highest bough."

"He's a smart man, that granddaddy of yours." I laughed and then took a deep breath, my stomach swimming with nerves. "My eternity belongs to you."

"What's that?" Asher stomped on the brake and put the truck into park. He looked over at me, happiness and hope filling his eyes.

"The engraving on the ring. That's what it says—'my eternity belongs to you.' It's an Elven eternity band."

His head bobbed in a slow nod as the pleased expression on his face grew. "You gave that to me *way* before you had any idea how all of this was going to turn out. So maybe you're not as scared as you think."

I released my belt and scooted across the seat into his waiting arms. "No, I'm pretty much terrified." I laughed.

"All right then." Asher plucked the ring from my fingertips and slid it onto my left hand. "Want to be terrified together?"

I looked into beautiful blue eyes that saw the truth about me and loved me anyway. "I do. I really do."

EPILOGUE

Instead of going to The Skillet for breakfast, Asher and I went back to his farm, taking the hidden rear entrance of course, to share the news with his granddaddy and his mom.

I found out what grits were—very tasty by the way—and I found out why Granddaddy had installed the underground perimeter defense to his property so many years ago.

"I grew up in the old country hearing stories of the Sidhe—or Fae folk—from my da and his da. Of course I never took any of it too seriously," he said. "That is until shortly after I moved to Deep River and bought this land and started clearing it for farming. I was felling a tree when a group of folks come walking through the woods, all dressed fine as you please, not like a hunting party or hikers. I told them hello and asked where they were going. They walked right up to me, not a one of them smiling. When they got close I felt sort of afraid, you ken, because they didn't look normal. They were fiercely beautiful. And some of them had on jewelry with strange symbols—like on that pretty ring of yours. I'll never forget the look of them. I was a bit frightened, like I said, but I told them 'hello' again, trying to be hospitable."

"They probably didn't understand you," I offered. "The Light Elves don't speak aloud as we do."

"Oh, they understood me well enough, lass—they had no interest in being neighborly. One of the three males in the group asked me what I was doing—more like he demanded to know. I explained I was clearing the land to farm it. And he said something about how it was typical of 'humans' to think they own the world and to alter it for their own selfish purposes. Well, by this time, I was getting pretty heated. I started to argue with him—I bought the land with my hard-earned money, and I needed to farm it to make a living. Then another fellow stepped forward."

He stopped and cut his gaze over to Asher. "Had the bluest eyes I'd ever seen in my life—like turquoise sea waters. He asked if I might consider leaving a swath of land untouched at the back of the property so he and his people could maintain their traditional traveling routes to and from a certain destination they had to reach every ten years. Well, it all sounded like mad daftie talk to me. I was about to tell him so when he said something that chilled me to my bones."

"What was it?" Asher asked, enrapt.

"He said, 'You would be wise to make this small concession, for the sake of your beautiful daughter.'"

Granddaddy passed a hand over his face, drawing a shaky breath. "Jenna was only eight years old at the time. She loved to play outside and run around and explore the property. Before that day I'd always thought of it as the safest place she could possibly be. I wasn't going to take any chances. I agreed to leave the woods untouched at the back of the property, and they went on their way. I started digging the trench that day—right inside the tree line. I wasn't sure if it would work or not, but it was the only thing I could think to do, short of moving. I'd sunk my life savings into the land—it was supposed to make a future for my family."

"And it worked?" Asher asked.

"It did," Granddaddy paused. "… for the most part."

"It still does, apparently," I said.

Asher wore a smug grin. "I don't think Culley will be too eager to come back for seconds. If he does—or if he sends someone else—I'll be ready for them. I'm going to talk to the guy down at the gun shop about making me some pure iron buckshot."

"He won't be back," I said. I was sure of it. I'd seen it in his eyes.

I wasn't the right person for Culley—I couldn't save him—from Audun, or from himself. And deep down inside, he knew it. In spite of the cocky threats he'd thrown at Asher, he had already let me go.

I only hoped—for his own sake—he'd eventually let *someone* else in.

AFTERWORD

Thank you for reading Hidden Danger! I really hope you enjoyed it. If you did, would you consider leaving a review at Amazon or wherever you bought your copy? And if your fingers aren't too tired, at Goodreads, too? Reviews are so important for authors and help other readers find great books.

There is more to come in the Hidden World. Book 6 of the saga, HIDDEN DESIRE, releases in September 2016. Here's the story:

Beauty is in the eye of the beholder...
Culley Rune is the perfect guy—as far as anyone can see. Inside, he knows he's unlovable, unworthy, unwanted. He's done terrible things in service to his father, the corrupt leader of the Dark Council—including playing a pivotal role in the mysterious new drug epidemic that's sweeping the human population of the world.

Now that he's lost his one chance at a real relationship, there's no reason to change his ways. He might as well take his place at his mercenary father's side. But when he runs into a strange human girl in the worst possible place at the worst possible time, he can't seem to stop himself from getting involved, and he may have found the one person on earth who can see past his beautiful facade to the heavily-guarded heart that lies beneath.

In this sixth book of the Hidden Saga, as the battle between the Dark and Light courts rages on, the fate of the human race may lie in Culley's hands, and the fate of his heart may rest with the last girl he'd ever have expected to breach his defenses.

Turn the page for a sneak preview of HIDDEN DESIRE...

HIDDEN DESIRE
CHAPTER ONE

What a hell hole.

This neighborhood is my least favorite district of L.A., and believe me, for a city with a reputation for beaches and sunshine and glittering movie premiers, it has *plenty* of areas you wouldn't want to be caught dead in. Actually—if you *were* caught in one of them and didn't belong there, you'd likely end up dead.

I walk past a seedy apartment building, a loud TV blaring from one of its screenless windows guarded by security bars. Behind a chain link fence across the street a couple of pit bulls bark and snarl at me as if they'd love to have me for an afternoon snack and leave no leftovers.

I have no fears for my own security. For one thing, I don't give a shit. For another, they want *me* here. I bring the only thing the lowlifes in this part of town still care about. Whatever good people are left here are no doubt cowering inside, hoping the "scourge" will pass them by.

At least the streets don't reek as much as they used to—fewer drunks puking up their paychecks into the gutters. S has nearly taken the place of booze, cocaine, heroin, and every other recreational drug in this city—it's cheaper than any of them and far more addictive.

I arrive at the pre-determined street corner and check my phone for the time—I'm early. Shit. I lean against the side of an auto repair shop that's closed for the day and check my messages, scrolling through the list of texts, opening none of them. I already know what they want, and it's a guarantee *all* of them want something from me. Everyone does.

Something moves near my feet, startling me and making me jump to the side. At first I think it's a rat, then I realize it's a gray cat—a young one—a kitten actually. It's filthy and so bony it hardly resembles a domestic animal at all.

When it realizes I've noticed it, the scrawny thing mewls at me.

"Go away," I bark at it, and the pitiful thing skitters back, then it takes a few cautious steps toward my shoes again.

I lift one foot and kick the air. "Get! I've got nothing for you. Go find a mouse or something." It makes another noise, louder this time. "Listen here—you want some advice? Don't count on anyone to give you anything in this life—the sooner you learn that one, the better."

The kitten is apparently smarter than most human beings—it runs away from me. I snort a laugh at my own expense. Wouldn't Ava be so proud?

I can't stop myself from thinking of our last conversation two months ago. *You'll never be happy until you let your guard down and open your heart and let someone see the real you,* she said. What a laugh. The real me is right here, passing on cynical life lessons to a flea bitten stray. And I'll *never* be happy. That possibility died the minute she told me she was in love with that human farm boy.

As far as my heart—I'm not sure I even have one. I've never felt the kind of emotion she seems to have for that silly dimpled bloke, the kind of attachment the Light King Lad and his bride seem to have for each other. And I don't want to. They're all destined for disappointment—they're just too dumb to know it.

The afternoon sun is in my eyes, so I back into a doorway for shade. I'd really rather not think of Ava at all. With that glamour of hers, the least she could have done was erase her bothersome self from my memory—would have been the kind thing to do. But then "kindness" has never been my fate. Indifference and lack of interference is about the best I can hope for.

Down the street, the kitten shows itself again, making a beeline for its next panhandling target—the critter is persistent, I'll give it that. Seeing its determination, I develop a grudging sense of admiration for the scrappy little beggar. Clearly it's fending for itself on these mean streets—its mum was probably killed by a car, or maybe she abandoned it. I know the feeling.

Good luck, Dogbait.

The kitten cautiously approaches a girl on the sidewalk. She's walking my way with a piece of paper in one hand, dragging the fingertips of the other along the side of the building next to her.

She's not the usual sort I see in this neighborhood. Quite the opposite actually. She's wearing a red sundress—and not one of those short, clingy kinds the girls wear to the clubs or for attracting *customers*. It's more of the go-on-a-picnic-to-the-park kind of dress. I can almost see her flying a kite in it or picking wildflowers or some nonsense like that.

She's got long straight sandy-brown hair—very clean looking—with a red headband holding it back from her face like freakin' Alice in Wonderland or something. She looks… proper. No, that's the wrong word. Innocent—that's it—almost like a primary schooler, but she's at least fifteen. Anyway, she stands out. Not a good thing around here.

I shrug. *It's your funeral, babe.*

I look down at my phone, but within a minute I find myself glancing up again. The girl has stopped walking. She's just standing there, turning in a slow circle with her head lifted. What the hell is she doing? And then it hits me. She's probably on S. That's what she's doing here—trying to score another hit. She's not the first dreamer from a small town to get off the bus in this city and get hooked on S right away.

The kitten reaches her and does a circle eight around her ankles. Immediately she stoops and picks it up, hugging it to her chest and smiling. I can't hear her, but she's obviously talking to the nasty little beast in her arms.

I shake my head and go back to my phone. *Stupid girl.* She and that mangy cat deserve one another. They can waste away together. She certainly won't be spending her money on cat food if she's hooked on S. There are suburban moms who don't feed their own children because they've blown the grocery money on the drug.

I blow out an aggravated breath. Five minutes until our meeting, and the guy hasn't shown yet. He'd better be here if he knows what's good for him. I'm not exactly thrilled about making a trip to this dump for no reason—especially since my "duties" usually take me to much more posh places, places where the drug addicts are much cleaner and more attractive. But I'm the least of this low level dealer's worries. My annoyance is nothing compared to Audun's wrath. He doesn't tolerate mistakes in his operation.

"Hey! Check this out."

I lift my head to see the owner of the very loud, very amused voice. It belongs to a heavyset, heavily tattooed man wearing a dirty white tank shirt and long, wide-legged shorts that expose all but the very bottom of his underwear. He's accompanied by two similarly dressed "gentlemen." Unlike the foolish girl in the red dress, they definitely fit this neighborhood.

The three men are laughing, striding down the center of the street directly toward her. "Little Red Riding Hood came to bring us some goodies, I think," one of them says in a lewd tone.

The third one joins in. "Wonder what she's got in *that* basket?" The laughter grows louder and more raucous.

My pulse kicks up a notch as I watch them pass my location in the doorway and approach the girl. She doesn't seem to notice, still too wrapped up in that pitiful cat or her S high, or maybe both.

A text tone draws my attention back to my phone. It's from my father. Great.

-Meeting location has changed. New location two blocks south. A bar called Moco's. Your contact is there now.

Naturally. The one day I'm early for a delivery, and my contact changes locations on me. I push forward out of the doorway and start down the street to where my car is parked. I'm ready to get this thing over with and get out of here before the locals decide to start helping themselves to some high end automotive parts. I've got more deliveries to make and in far more pleasant locales than this one.

"Hey, hey little girl. You lost or something?"

"Grandma's house is that way. Better watch out for the wolf."

Don't look. It doesn't matter. It's not your concern. Humans preying on other humans—happens all day every day all over the globe.

I will my eyes forward but they veer off to the left without my consent. The street thugs have reached Alice, as I've dubbed her. She's standing with her back to the wall now, the stupid cat cradled in her arms. The guys move in close to her, forming a human triangle around her. One of

275

them tugs at her dress, and she spins to face him. She doesn't look particularly afraid, but she's not looking directly at any of them.

And you shouldn't be either, moron. You've got a job to do. Keep walking.

I stop walking.

Blowing out a long breath of resignation, I turn toward the scene on the sidewalk. As if possessed by a mind of their own, my feet start moving in that direction. My hands clench at my sides, tightening by increments the closer I get.

I'm not sure exactly what I plan to do when I get there. A couple of the guys are shorter than me, so I'd have the reach on them in a fistfight, but all three are considerably heavier. And in this neighborhood, probably armed. And did I mention there are *three* of them?

In spite of these very valid reasons to walk the other way, I don't. Instead, when I reach the sidewalk, I step right up to the group and through the stinking, tattooed human chain surrounding the girl.

She's older than I thought—maybe about eighteen. Prettier, too. Now that I get a good look at her, I can tell she's not high. She is frightened though. She's staring right at the sweat stain on the t-shirt of one of the guys, not making eye contact with any of them or with me. Her chest rises and falls with quick, shallow breaths. She's probably catatonic with fear by this point.

Reaching for the ugly gray kitten, I say, "There you are, naughty kitty. Thank you, love, for finding her. I've been looking for little Tinkerbell everywhere."

"Who the hell are you?" the tallest of the guys demands.

"Well now I've just said that, haven't I? I'm the owner of Tinkerbell here."

"That cat's a *dude*, man. And he's running wild around here every day, begging for scraps."

"Even more reason I'm thrilled to have him back. Now I must be going. And I'll need the young lady to come with me. You see I filed a police report on my missing cat, and she'll need to come in and give a statement that she returned him to me and did not, in fact, steal Tinkerbell. Someone might have witnessed her holding him and reported her already."

One of the shorter guys laughs. "That's bullshit man. The cops around here don't care about no missing cats."

"Better safe than sorry," I say and slide an arm around the girl's back, steering her toward the street. She's trembling and so is the kitten. "We're going to my car," I mutter to the girl. "Just come along and I'll drop you somewhere safe."

Her feet stop moving. "I don't want to leave."

What? How stupid is this girl? Or are people really *that* naïve where she's from? "Don't argue," I urge under my breath. "Believe me—you *want* to leave—unless you particularly relish the prospect of gang rape and human trafficking."

"Oh," she says and starts moving again.

"Hey—English dude."

Great. "Keep walking," I say to the girl, tucking the cat under her arm again. I turn to face the delayed reaction of the neighborhood gang, who've finally realized I'm whisking their new toy away. "Yes?"

"We didn't say she could leave. We were just getting to know Little Red there."

"Yes well, I believe the young lady may be lost, and the last thing guys with your records need is a lost tourist disappearing on your turf—especially one who looks like this one. Now *there's* something the cops *will* care about. All of you ready to have your houses and cars thoroughly searched?"

The three men exchange glances. The answer visible on all of their faces is a definitive "No." My guess about their prison records was apparently spot on. Still, the leader of the group doesn't like that I've defied him in front of his underlings.

He sticks his barrel chest out and curls his lips into a nasty smile. "Wonder if they'd care about a smart-mouth English guy with his ass beat in?"

I release a weary breath. "I'm from Australia, actually, and this conversation is getting tedious." Eager to get the girl out of there and get to my meeting, I put a heavy dose of Sway into my next words. "Now you're gonna turn around, walk back over to your men, and order them to follow you. Then the three of you will walk to the farthest edge of your 'territory' and pick a fight with someone closer to your own size—preferably a member of a rival gang. This city could use a few less hoodlums. Have a nice day, *gentlemen*."

The guy stares at me a second, then turns and shows me his back, gesturing to his men.

"Come on. We outta here," he says.

Turning back toward the girl, I pick up my pace to catch up with her. Though I instructed her to keep walking, she's not far from where I left her. I grab her upper arm and move quickly, pulling her along by my side.

"Let's go before any of the Three Amigos' friends get a look at you and start coming out of the woodwork. It's almost dark—and you think this place is bad during the daytime, you do *not* want to see it at night."

She nods and silently stumbles along beside me, clutching the kitten, clearly still in shock from her near miss. We reach my car, I pop the door locks and open hers. She puts a hand on the door and lowers herself inside. I close the door and go around to the driver's side, sliding in and starting the car, not even waiting for the engine to warm before putting it in gear and driving straight past Moco's and out of the neighborhood. Chesterfield can live without its S fix for one night.

When we make it to the 110 onramp and merge into traffic I finally breathe normally. And then I let her have it.

"*What* were you thinking going there? Are you stupid? Are you *blind*? Anyone can see that's no place for someone like you."

Her little chin juts out as she stares straight ahead through the windshield, holding the kitten to her chest where it's attempting to burrow into her. "I paid a lot of money for a taxi ride to take me there."

My jaw drops. Maybe I was wrong. Maybe she *was* there searching for a fix after all. But why go there? She could score S in almost any nightclub in the city. I glance over at her curled up in my passenger seat. She doesn't look like the typical S addict. Her skin is smooth and clear, her hair shines. She has all her teeth—white and strong. Her hands aren't shaking and her eyes, though still a bit dazed looking, aren't bloodshot or rimmed with dark shadows. In fact, they're a beautiful clear brown with spokes of greenish-gold.

She's not a junkie. Maybe she really *is* that naïve. "As you may have noticed from your encounter with the hood welcoming committee back there, that was *not* a good neighborhood. And when you saw those guys coming... you should have run."

The chin tilts higher. "If it's such a bad neighborhood, what were you doing there? Maybe *you're* a bad guy. Maybe I should have run from *you*."

Her sassy attitude is a surprise. I chuckle. "Without a doubt. I am a very bad guy indeed. But I'm also the guy who got your silly little arse out of danger, so I believe a thank you is in order."

"Thank you," she says. And that's all she says.

"Well, now that we've established your *undying* gratitude for my *saving your life*," I drawl. "Tell me where you live—I'll take you home."

"You don't have to do that—you can just drop me off anywhere. I'll catch a bus."

"Don't be daft. Look—I was sort of joking about that being a bad guy thing. Tell me where your apartment is. I promise not to stalk you. I won't even try to walk you to the door—I'll just slow down and you can jump out," I joke.

There's a long pause before she answers. "I don't have an apartment."

"Your hotel then, friend's house—whatever."

"I don't have one of those either. I was planning to look for a place near the clinic. That's why I went to South Los Angeles."

"Excuse me?"

I pull the car off at the next exit simply so I can get a look at her face and see if she's joking. Also, my hands have begun to shake. After steering the car into a convenience store lot and putting it in park, I turn in my seat to face her. The expression she wears is entirely serious. She's not kidding. Which means she's insane.

"You can't mean the S clinic. The one next door to the *drug den*. Why in God's name would you look for an apartment *there*? You're not using are you?"

"No." She laughs. "No, I'm going to work there—as a volunteer. I spoke to them on the phone before coming out to Los Angeles. I don't drive, so I need a place that's nearby. I can't afford to keep taking taxis."

I don't know why, but this girl's insistence on putting her life at risk in that drug-infested neighborhood is driving me nuts. She's clearly unfamiliar with the area. What is she *doing* out here all alone? Doesn't anyone realize she's far too naïve to even be in the *good* parts of this city? Where are her parents? Where are her friends?

My fingertips dig into the back of her seat. "Look at me please."

At first she doesn't move, but then she slowly turns her face toward me.

"What is your name?" I ask.

"Laney."

"Laney what?"

She opens her mouth but hesitates. Finally she says, "Just Laney. What's yours?"

"Culley Rune. And where are you from, Just Laney?" *Because I'm going to make it my personal mission to send you back there—today if possible.*

She must be reading my mind because she gives me a vague answer. "The Midwest."

"Where exactly?"

"You ask a lot of questions."

"I'm a curious guy." I wait for a more specific answer until it's clear she's not going to give one. "Okay fine. I'm taking you to a hotel in a *safe* area for tonight. Tomorrow, you're going to get on a bus or a plane or a train or however the hell you got out here from *wherever* the hell you're from, and you're going back there where you belong before you get yourself hurt or worse."

I expect anger, defiance, or maybe resignation if I'm lucky. But there's none of that in her eyes. She gazes at me with the strangest expression.

Ah, I know what this is. I'm used to it by now. While some humans respond to my physical appearance with immediate lust or desire in their eyes, others are thrown off balance by the sensory input. It's an effect of my glamour.

But then… this one is different somehow. I can't quite put my finger on it.

"No thank you," she says sweetly. "All the hotels out here are pretty expensive. You know what? Just drop me off at one of the beaches, and I'll sleep there tonight. I like the feel of the sand, and with the sound of the ocean it'll be like falling asleep to my sound machine in my room back home."

"That—is ridiculous." I don't understand why, but I can feel my blood pressure rising. The temperature inside the car has increased by at least fifteen degrees in the last minute. I lower the windows, letting in some air and the sounds of traffic from the nearby street.

"You can't sleep on the beach." I jam my hand into my back pocket and draw out my wallet, ripping a couple of hundreds from it and jabbing them at her. "I'll *pay* for the hotel." Delving back in again, I pull out more bills. "In fact, here—have a plane ticket on me."

Her fingers extend toward mine, passing over the money, seeking and finding my skin. She squeezes my hand briefly then lets it go.

"Thank you. Really. But I'm fine. I don't need your money or your pity. I can take care of myself." She pauses and smiles. "You know, I believe I will call a cab after all. You've been so kind, and I don't want to trouble you any further."

I'm being dismissed. She doesn't want my help. She doesn't want my money. Hell, she doesn't even want a ride from me. Who *is* this girl?

The sound of my phone's ringer startles me, making me realize I've been staring at her face. That's a first—I'm usually the recipient of human stares, not the other way around. I pick up my phone and check the screen. It's my father. *Damn it.*

"I have to answer this. Hold on." I hold up a finger to her to signal that our conversation is not over yet.

Ignoring the gesture, Laney puts one hand on the door handle, preparing to get out of the car. She turns back to me. "Thank you for what you did today." Then she leans close for a conspiratorial whisper. "You might not think you're one of the good guys, Culley Rune—but you're wrong."

Then she brushes my cheek with a soft kiss and opens the door, stepping out onto the sidewalk. Blinking against a feeling of sudden disorientation, I answer the phone.

"Yes, Father?" My eyes follow Laney to the end of the block where she stops at the corner. I lift my hand and scratch the place her lips touched my face, attempting to erase the lingering sensation they left behind. It's a strange tingling, an annoying warm tickle like nothing I've never felt before.

"You *missed* your drop." Audun's every word is imbued with a menace that would no doubt make the rest of his underlings tremble. Luckily, I've been inoculated with small doses my entire life, so it has a lesser effect on me.

"Yes Father."

"Well? What happened? Our associate waited as long as he was comfortable, and then he got nervous and left. That is *unacceptable*. What is your explanation?"

Through the windshield I watch Laney step up to the crossing sign pole and slide her hand down its side until she reaches the signal button, apparently intending to cross the street. To where? I thought she was calling a cab. Where is she going? Does she even know where she is?

"Culley?"

"I… got busy. I apologize. It won't happen again."

He snorts. "I should hope not. The last thing you need is *another* failure."

I roll my eyes at his reference to Ava and our bonding-that-never-happened. Naturally I can't let on that I lied about it without his realizing it. It's the one card I have in my pocket with him. It's better for me if he doesn't figure out I'm immune to his lie detecting glamour. So I told him Ava had used her glamour on me to make me *believe* we had bonded, when we actually had not. And then she had disappeared into thin air after our engagement ring commercial shoot.

He was infuriated by my "weakness" of course and ordered me to find her. I told him she must have removed most of my memories of her as well because I had no idea where to even begin looking.

"I'll make the delivery first thing tomorrow," I promise him.

The walk signal starts flashing in the pedestrian walkway sign, accompanied by a piercing beep for the visually impaired. Laney begins to step out into the crosswalk.

"Listen, I need to go. I'll speak with you tomorrow."

I hang up, already opening my car door and leaping out. Because I've figured out why Laney wasn't properly afraid of that godforsaken neighborhood, and why she never looked those thugs in the eye, and why when she looked at me, she wasn't glamoured like everyone else.

She couldn't see me.

She couldn't see any of it.

Laney is blind.

* * *

HIDDEN DESIRE releases in September 2016 and will be available for pre-order soon! Be among the first to find out what happens next in the Hidden world and never miss a new release from Amy Patrick by visiting her website and signing up for her newsletter. You will only receive notifications when new titles are available and about special price promotions. You may also occasionally receive teasers, excerpts, and extras from upcoming books. Amy will never share your contact information with others.

And check out http://www.thehiddensaga.com/ for more goodies on the Hidden series.

The Hidden Saga

Hidden Deep

Hidden Heart

Hidden Hope

The Sway, A Hidden Saga Companion Novella

Hidden Darkness

Hidden Danger

HIDDEN DESIRE- coming in Sept 2016

ABOUT THE AUTHOR

 Amy Patrick grew up in Mississippi (with a few years in Texas thrown in for spicy flavor) and has lived in six states, including Rhode Island, where she now lives with her husband and two sons.

She's been a professional singer, a DJ, a voiceover artist, and always a storyteller, whether it was directing her younger siblings during hours of "pretend" or inventing characters and dialogue while hot-rolling her hair before middle school every day. For many years she was a writer of true crime, medical anomalies, and mayhem, working as a news anchor and health reporter for six different television stations. Then she retired to make up her own stories. Hers have a lot more kissing.

I love to hear from my readers. Feel free to contact me on Instagram, Twitter and my Facebook page (where I hang out the most.) And be sure to sign up for my newsletter and be the first to hear the latest news from the Hidden world as well as other new books I have in the works!

ACKNOWLEDGMENTS

It is such an amazing thing for me to be closing out the fifth book in the Hidden Saga. I can't tell you how much I appreciate your love for this series and all the encouragement I get from my readers. Thank you for giving my books a chance to entertain you and touch your heart. I hope you will continue to love living in the Hidden world as much as I do!

Huge thanks go to my lovely editor Judy Roth for her wonderful work as always and to Cover Your Dreams for another brilliant cover.

I am forever grateful for my amazing critique partner, McCall, for her words of wisdom and huge heart. I'd be nowhere without my brilliant and hilarious Savvy Seven sisters, and I count so much on my Darling Dreamweavers and my Lucky 13 sisters for their support, good advice, virtual Prosecco, cupcakes, and cabana boys. #teamworddomination. I'm so proud of you all!

I'm blessed to be "doing life" with some amazing friends. Love to Bethany, Chelle, Margie, and the real housewives of Westmoreland Farm. Special thanks to Mary for the walks and talks and pots of tea.

To my first family for your unconditional love and the gift of roots and wings. And finally to the guys who make it all worthwhile—my husband and sons. And thank you to the rest of my friends and family for your support and for just making life good.

52518547R00177

Made in the USA
Middletown, DE
10 July 2019